ENCOUNTER WITH THE DEVIL

MAYA DANIELS

This book is a work of fiction. Any references, real places, real events, or real persons names and/or persona are used fictitiously. Everything in this story comes from the author's imagination and any similarities, whatsoever, with events both past and present, or persons living or dead, are purely coincidental.

Cover design by Jessica Allain, Enchanted Whispers

Interior design by Jessica Allain and Zoe Parker

Edited by Cassandra Fear

If you are unable to order paperback copy of this book from your local bookseller, you may contact the author at info@authormayadaniels.com or visit the website

www.authormayadaniels.com

Encounter with the Devil

Maya Daniels

Chapter One

Helena

The slight breeze, a faint scent of caramel making my mouth water, and the silvery moonlight were not the things I expected to see when dropping down to Hell, unannounced. After falling through an endless abyss for what felt like hours, my body passed through an invisible barrier before my tailbone took the brunt of the impact when I hit the packed-dirt ground. For whatever reason, I expected to jump in the gaping hole in the middle of Sanctuary and fall to the center of the Earth with lava licking at my heels.

As you might suspect by now, that is not the case.

Glancing at Eric from the corner of my eye tells me I'm still missing something. The unease is made stronger by the gnawing feeling in my gut and the involuntary tremble in my hands.

Holy shit, I'm in Hell!

My mind screams like that annoying girl in a horror movie, the one we all want to tell to shut up, while my body is standing as still as a statue expecting an attack at any moment. You can't just decide to drop in here and expect no one to notice, right?

"You okay?" Reaching for me, Eric tucks me under his shoulder. "You seem shocked."

"Ummm…kinda." With great effort, I pull my gaze away from my surroundings to look at him. "I'm not sure what I was expecting, but this"—Waving a hand to encompass everything, I let it drop to my side limply—"was not it."

"No, pitchforks?" Chuckling, his green eyes dance with amusement.

"No, no pitchforks." My snickering sounds strained. "Now what?"

He does a visual inspection while lines form in neat rows on his forehead. "We ended up further from the portal that we passed through than I expected." Rubbing the back of his neck, his frown deepens. "I was too worried about you to pay closer attention. It must've picked up on my bloodline and spit us out here."

"Is that a good thing or a bad thing?" Gut tightening,

my head swivels left and right, expecting a horde of demons to descend on us at any moment. “Your face is not giving me the warm fuzzies right now.”

Lips quirking on one side, Eric looks down at me. “I thought you liked my face.”

“Just 'cause you are pretty doesn’t mean I’m all happy to get my butt handed to me here.” His grin grows, and my hand itches to smack it off him. “Plus, you are stalling. Where are we, and how do we get out of here?”

“You picked up on that, huh.” With a sigh, he turns in half a circle. “We need to head north. At the moment, we are too close to Lucifer’s quarters. I would rather be away from here before he senses my presence.”

“Why are we standing here, chatting? Let’s go.” Pulling away from him, picking a direction, my feet move fast.

“Aren’t you forgetting something?”

Turning around, I keep walking backward with an eyebrow raised in question. Eric points to his right, and I follow the direction of his finger. My ability to see in the dark is not as good as his, but there is no mistaking the glint of the blade reflecting the glow of the moon. My feet stop like they’ve been nailed on the packed dirt, the bottom of my stomach dropping. A quick glance tells me Eric is forcing himself to stay rooted to the spot, his outstretched arm slightly twitching from the effort. Unwilling to test theories or ask questions when all I want to do is get out of here, my body moves so fast I’m almost sprinting. Snatching the dagger, tucking it at the small of my back, I turn to him.

"Got it, let's go."

His mouth opens, whatever he was about to say is lost in the sharp intake of breath, and his head snaps to the left; I'm surprised I didn't hear his neck breaking. Amber overtakes the green color of his eyes, and the unnatural stiffening of his body causes alarms to blare in my head. My own questions get strangled, forming a lump in my throat when a whooshing sound like helicopter blades reaches my ears.

They have helicopters in Hell? my mind supplies right before I'm tackled to the ground.

With a loud oomph, all the oxygen exits my lungs, my head spinning when Eric rolls us to the nearest tree. The blade digs into the skin of my back, luckily not severing my spine. Ending up on top of Eric at the gnarled roots of an ancient tree, I lift my head, pushing the hair out of my face. The area where we were standing looks like a circle clearing, surrounded by thorned bushes and rock formations; I didn't pay close attention to until now. From the place where I'm sprawled on top of a firm, warm body, I can tell it was made on purpose, and is not a natural formation as I previously assumed. Gray swirls resembling some of the markings on my blade are etched into the rocks, forming a tribal-looking art around the empty space in the middle. Ancient trees surround it on three sides, leaving the front open to a vast horizon that reminds me of old Earth. A time when technology and people haven't destroyed the beauty of nature around us. Dirt paths spread through tall trees, splitting in different directions, like veins forking under pale skin. The bright silver glow makes everything look enchanted, sparkling like jewels under the giant full orb in the sky. A starless sky, now that I'm focused on it.

Eric pulls me closer, wrapping his large hand around the back of my head, pressing my face in the crook of his neck. His arms are like steel bands around me, the stiffness more noticeable now that I'm touching him. My stupid body doesn't understand the panic that is filling my every pore. Eric is still shirtless from his wings bursting out of his back before we ended up in this mess. I become acutely aware of hard planes and muscles pressed to me from shoulder to groin, his hips wedged between my spread thighs. Warmth pools in my lower belly, and the scent of his skin where my nose is pressed to his neck hitches my breath.

I'm acutely aware of the moment his breath stops, his attention turning from whatever made him put us in this position to me. A deep rumble vibrates from his chest to mine, and I can hear him sniffing me. "Bad timing, Hel. Tone it down, or we might get caught with me buried inside you."

That's one way to throw a bucket of ice-cold water on a girl's libido. Muscles clenching in anticipation of whatever he sensed coming for us, I jerk my head up, but he holds me firmly where I am.

"No one wants to get caught with their pants around their ankles." My words are muffled, the chuckle falling flat. "You need to find a shirt to put on."

"Right after I get us out of here." His whispered promise is met with a louder whooshing sound.

The temperature around us goes up by a few degrees. Sweat starts trickling between my shoulder blades, leaving my hair plastered to my skin and Eric's shoulders. Blasts of hot air keep hitting my back in waves and the strangest thought barrels through my head. *Why am I on top of Eric? He always shields me using his own body. Now it seems like he is using me for a living shield.* Pushing the stupid idea to the back of my mind, I strain my ears to decipher what's making the sound.

Whoosh, whoosh, whoosh.

There is a pause between the sound and the blast of scorching heat burning every inch of exposed skin. If it keeps going, I have no doubt I'm going to blister from head to toe. Heart jackhammering in sync with the men underneath me, I grind my teeth so I don't utter a sound. It's not every day I see Eric hiding instead of bulldozing his way through whatever stands in his way. That's enough to hold me frozen, even if it means I'll burn to a crisp under the barrage of what feels like an open furnace at my back.

After a long time, when I'm sure I'll be spending days

laying on my stomach to protect my burned back, the heat starts dissipating along with the whooshing sound that is getting further away from us. Eric loosens his hold on me but doesn't push me off him. Curiosity is stronger than the agonizing pain in my back, and with great effort, I lift my head, looking up where I can see the starless sky. A shadow large enough to almost cover the entire span of the pregnant silver moon makes me suck in a sharp breath. I regret it the same second when an excruciating stinging pain stabs my back. Regardless of it all, my eyes must be as round and as big as the moon above me. After the shadow banks left and disappears in the distance, my stunned gaze drops down to Eric. He is watching me like he expects me to pull my blade and cut his throat. Swallowing the bile that's trying to push its way through my esophagus, my eyes lift up to where I saw the shadow last.

Hell has motherfucking dragons. More extensive than a helicopter, with a fire burning along their spine and wings; those type of dragons.

And no one thought this little information to be significant enough to be the first thing they mentioned.

Chapter Two

"We are going to die!" whisper-yelling at Eric, I push myself off him, hissing in pain.

"What's wrong?" Lifting on his knees, he grabs my arm when I try to move away from him.

"It looks like we might have to lay low until I heal." Jerking back like I've slapped him, Eric's fingers go slack where they wrap around my arm. "I'm not sure I can move much before that."

"Heal…" his words trail off, and before I realize what he is doing, I'm flipped around, so my back is turned towards him. "Where are you hurt? Did I hurt you?"

“What did you think was going to happen when all that heat was blasted our way, Eric?” Frustrated at his manhandling, I shrug off his touch. “We are lucky the trees didn’t catch fire forcing us out in the open, blistered skin or not.”

“You felt heat?” Glancing at him over my shoulder, my anger bleeds away at his shocked expression. “Your skin is not burned.”

Slowly, I turn to face him again, grateful we are still under the protection of the trees when I have no idea what else is waiting for us after we emerge. “That’s good news. It will take less time until I can move.” My words cut off when he shakes his head at me, rubbing a hand over his face.

“The dragon, as you call it, has an ability to alter your mind and force your fears to the front. It’s easier to capture prey if it’s scared and can’t think logically. There was never any heat around us because it was too high in the air for you to be able to feel it.” Meshing his lips in a firm flat line, the disappointment in his gaze feels like a physical punch to my sternum. “You think I would ever place you in front of me to protect myself if that means you’d be harmed?”

Considering the fact I was rescued from a building that exploded around me, fear from burning alive might’ve come to mind once or twice. “It did cross my mind that the situation was strange, but I was too busy making sure I didn't scream out in pain to give it more thought." The longer we talk, the less I feel the stinging on my back. "It's not like I had time to consider options, or even think before we were eating dirt at the roots of this tree."

His mouth opens, only a rush of air passing his lips when he keeps whatever words he wanted to say to himself. As I search his face, I can feel the walls lifting up behind his eyes, hiding him from me and closing off the Eric I know. Like a gaping chasm, the distance between us grows, regardless that we are physically so close our knees are almost touching. I don't feel bad for having doubts, especially when everyone handles me like a fragile piece of glass that can shatter at any moment. It doesn't mean seeing him distance himself from me hurts any less.

"We need to move." Lifting himself up, he reaches for my hand. "That won't be the only thing searching the area now that they've picked up on me being back here."

"Picked up you're here?" Allowing him to pull me to my feet, I wiggle my shoulders, testing the tightness of the skin that still lingers. Having my mind preoccupied with other things helps push away whatever that thing did to my brain. "Your father knows we are in Hell?"

"It would appear so, yes." With one last searching look, he turns away and walks out from the cover of the trees around us.

I watch him go, my mind swirling with guilt that I shake off with determination. He can't blame me for having doubts when everyone I've known has betrayed me, one way or another. Reaching behind me, I check that the dagger is still nestled at the small of my back before I follow behind Eric. His shoulders are stiff, although he is not walking fast enough to leave me too far behind. With a sigh, I turn around in a circle, checking the symbols etched on the rocks in the clearing before hurrying to catch up to him.

Avoiding the tension thrumming between us, I scan the area, trying to see everything at once. Dangerous calm that can get you killed surrounds me like we are the only two people in this entire realm. No birds are chirping, no rustling of leaves. Just a soft, warm breeze and sparkling moonlight as far as my eyes can see. My warning GPS has been surprisingly quiet considering that I'm in Hell. Shouldn't it go haywire warning me of the danger I'm in? It didn't even stir when that terrifying dragon was above me. The guilt for doubting Eric even for a short moment stabs me in the gut. Clearing my throat, I finally break the silence between us.

"I didn't feel any danger."

Eric's feet falter for a second before he resumes his clipped pace, not turning to look at me. "What do you mean?"

Panic clogs my throat, and the thought of talking about something I've kept hidden most of my life tries to choke me, so I stay silent. The longer I say nothing, the more his gait slows down until I can touch his back if I reach my hand out. My fingers twitch with the need to do just that, but I clench a fist at my side. Being a hypocrite has never been so glaringly evident until this moment. I hold it against everyone for hiding things from me, yet it's not like I'm an open book, is it? Swallowing the unease trying to choke me, I lift my face up towards the moon, looking for comfort. Eric doesn't push or barrage me with questions. He never does, I realize. He is simply there, allowing me to pick my comfort zone to share what I'm ready to share with him, and nothing more.

"I've always had this thing," my words are murmured under my breath, but I know he hears me. I can see his head turn my way from the corner of my eye. "I call it my GPS." Chuckling awkwardly, I look away from the moon and let my hair fall around my face to hide me from his penetrating gaze. "It's a feeling I get in the center of my chest when my life is in danger. On all my hunts, it has saved my life more than once. I associate it with evil being near since it was only activated around demons." My eyebrows pull down after those words are said out loud. "It's been getting wonky lately. I felt it around the holy ass a couple of times, but not always while he kept me prisoner. And it stayed silent a moment ago when that dragon thing was above our heads."

Eric says nothing, just the crunching of dirt under our feet breaking the silence. Lifting my head up, I glance at him, but he is not looking at me. With a thoughtful expression, he is scanning our surroundings. Maybe he didn't even hear what I said, which is a good thing. I shouldn't have shared it. Adding stuff to the pile of crazy that makes me who I am is never a good idea. My heart skips a beat when he finally speaks.

"How does it feel?" At my questioning look, he finally turns those green eyes on me. "When your GPS gets activated, how does it feel?" A quirk of his lips is the only glimpse that my Eric is still there beneath the invisible armor he donned, but it's gone too fast for me to feel any better.

"It's a warning." The lie, tasting bitter on my tongue, is clear as a day in this realm covered in darkness. I can feel Eric watching me as if saying, "Really? You're going to go with that?" Filling my lungs with as much air as they can hold, I release it slowly, like a wheezing balloon after you stick a needle in it. "It makes me feel excited, okay? Like I'm about to receive the gift of a lifetime." Wiping my sweaty palms on my pants, I don't dare turn his way. "Like I wasn't a freak enough without it."

His large hand takes my sweaty one, and he laces our fingers together. Until this moment, I wasn't aware of the heavy burden sitting on my chest from the disappointment I saw in his eyes. My entire body sags and I stumble, his hold on my hand the only thing stopping me from face-planting in the dirt.

"Come here." With a jerk on my arm, he pulls me in

the circle of his arms. I grip him tightly like a lifeline, my fingers digging in the skin of his back. "No matter what I say, or how many times I say it, you can't stop seeing yourself as a freak." Sinking his face in my hair, he inhales deeply, pressing his chest firmly to mine. "Maybe one day you'll believe me."

"I'm sorry." My apology is muffled, his skin pebbling where my lips touch it when I speak. Not waiting for him to ask the obvious question, I keep talking, getting it out without having to look at his face. "I know you'll never put me in danger, or use me as a shield to protect yourself. You've proven that from the first moment I saw you. That's why I found it strange having you beneath me while danger loomed over our heads. And it was never an accusing thought just a fleeting one considering the situation we were in. I don't doubt you, Eric." Finally pulling away, I lift my face up to see him. "I just can't help the thoughts floating through my head when everyone I've ever loved and called family has betrayed me. It's not something I can control. Not yet, anyway…maybe never."

"I'll just have to try harder, so you'll never have a doubt in your mind when it comes to me, Hel." After kissing the tip of my nose, he leans his chin on top of my head. "I've failed as a mate when it comes to protecting you, and that's all on me. I haven't shared myself openly with another either. I know it's not easy for you because it's not easy for me. We will figure it out. Together."

"Together…" Warmth spreads through my body when

I whisper it back to him. Opening my mouth to say something I haven't mentioned until now, the L gets stuck in my throat when his body stiffens.

"We have company." Faster than I can blink, he pulls us into the cover of the trees lining the path.

Chapter Three

I'm more freaked out by the fact I was going to tell Eric that I loved him than I am from whatever is coming our way. He blends with the shadows, the darkness welcoming him like it's an extension of who he is. Pressing my back to the tree, I watch him a few feet away, only the amber glow of his eyes separating him from the cloak of darkness surrounding us. Long moments pass, and just when I think he made a mistake, I hear the distant chatter and crunching of feet on the path. My hand grabs the blade, sliding it out from the waistband holding it secure at my lower back.

In the stillness around us, even my breath sounds too loud to my own ears. Parting my lips, I breathe through my mouth, the closer the shuffling gets to where we are. Eric points at the thicker cluster of trees, his unspoken demand for me to move there irking me to no end. With a quick jerk of my head, I tell him what I think of his idea while lifting the blade slightly, just enough for him to see it. I can feel his frustration pulsing off him, and a grin splits my face. The damn GPS stays silent. Winking at him, the calm I always feel before I start hunting blankets me from head to toe. His eyes burn brighter, hunger unmistakable in their depths, but the noises are almost upon us, so I push the fluttering butterflies in my stomach away.

"Move, you useless piece of shit." A thump follows raspy words, then something hits the dirt path and a soft cry makes my whole body clench. "This is your last chance to prove your worth before I suck you dry." Chuckles echo around us, drowning a soft whimper.

Inching my way as close as I dare to the edge of the wide tree trunk, I glance at the path. My lungs shrivel when I see two hunched ogre-looking demons kicking the tiny body of a little boy at their feet. His pants are ripped and dirty, his ribs protruding through the skin of his bare torso while his fingers dig in the dirt so he can crawl away from them. The tasseled curls on his head fall over, hiding his face from me. My body moves without conscious thought. A twisting shadow gives me the warning to brace myself before my back gets slammed harshly to the tree again. Eric clamps his paw-sized hand over my mouth, cutting off anything I would've said.

And there is a lot I want to say to him right now.

Looking down at me, he shakes his head, my glare not deterring him one little bit. There is no way I'm going to hide in the shadows while demons are hurting the boy. Lucifer himself can come for my head if he wants, but I'll be damned if I allow him or Eric to stop me. Anger burns like a raging fire inside me, the ground at my feet trembling along with it. Lately, I've been too fast to anger, the switch flipping without warning, but another whimper coming from somewhere behind the tree doesn't give me the time to ponder that for long. Placing my free hand at the center of Eric's chest, I shove him away like he weighs nothing. His eyes widen comically. I'm already moving, not giving him time to recover and stop me.

"Step away from the boy." Stepping in their path, my knees bend slightly, preparing for a fight. Adrenaline pumps through my veins, making me bounce slightly on the balls of my feet.

"What have we here?" the demon on the left rasps, his square head canting to the side like he is watching a bug under his shoe. "I have not seen the likes of you around here, girly. Where did you come from?"

His skin has a stone-like appearance, flakes falling off it with his movements, like the peeling paint of an old house. The lump on his back combined with his hunched down posture, does not make him any smaller. He still towers over me, forcing me to crane my neck so I can look at his ugly face. Broad set eyes, all black with no iris or pupil, scrutinize me. Nostrils flare, pulling my attention to his flattened nose sitting above a slit on his face, which serves as a mouth if the rows of sharp, yellowed teeth are any indication. The one next to him looks the same, only a few clusters of hair like weeds on his boxed head allowing me to tell the difference.

"I said, 'step away from the boy.'" My voice is calm, and I scan them both, looking for vulnerable spots where I can stick the dagger gripped in my hand.

"We don't have time for this." The demon with weed for hair waves his trunk-like arm around. "The portal will close if we linger. Grab her and let's go."

The slit on the face of the other one grows, showing off more teeth than any mouth should hold. Sidestepping the tiny body curled up at his feet, he moves towards me. His friend bends down, grabbing the boy by the arm, hauling him up in the air. No sound comes from the kid while he hangs limply in the air. Gut tight with worry because I might be too late makes me jump at the demon as soon as he is within reach. Not expecting me to go at something like him like a battering ram, he takes a step back when we collide. Using his surprise to my advantage, I slash the dagger in an arc across his throat. His head glides off his shoulders, landing with a thud on the ground. The large body follows, gravity pulling it down, and I ride him with my knees pressed on his stomach like a surfboard. A loud thump and a cloud of dust are the only sound he will ever make again.

Jumping off the dead demon, I roll away from his stunned friend before bouncing on my feet, blocking his way. “I said, ‘let the boy go.’”

“You fucking bitch!” the demon roars, throwing the boy away from him and charging at me.

Praying that the kid is still alive and won’t be hurt more than he already is, I brace for the impact. This is going to hurt. A hand larger than my head swings my way, and I drop on the ground, rolling away from him. The good thing about large creatures like this demon is that when they swing with all their strength, they can’t alter the direction of their hit. He stumbles for a few feet before he catches himself. Flipping around, his head swivels as he looks for me. Rage burns in his gaze, like molten lava spitting sparks, when it locks on mine. Pushing myself off the ground, I smile at him.

“Playtime, motherfucker.”

He charges me again at my taunting words.

“Enough!”

Eric’s shout freezes the demon mid-stride. I never thought a gray skin could pale, but I’m a believer now that I see the color draining from the demons face. In my urge to save the boy, I never for a second wondered where Eric was and why he didn’t join me. Black blood drips from my dagger and spreads around the headless body between the three of us.

“Shadow.” The demon drops on one knee, bowing his head. “You can have her if you wish. I mean no harm.”

My jaw hits my chest and I straighten. This is all he has to do to save the boy? My hands tremble at my side, the dagger warming under my tight hold from the anger overtaking me. So I don’t end up sticking the blade in the center of Eric’s forehead, I turn around and stomp towards the boy. For his sake, I hope the kid is alive. There would be no going back for us if he stood there behind the trees while demons killed a child. Dropping on my knees next to the heap on the ground, I tuck the dagger at the small of my back, shuddering when the sticky blood touches my skin.

“Helena, don’t!” Eric calls out, but I already have the boy lifted up so that he is sitting in front of me. After pushing the curls off his face, I scramble away from him like a crab on all fours, my butt scraping the dirt.

Sockets blackened, like the eyes were burned out of his head, are staring unseeing at me. I would’ve thought the creature was dead if he wasn’t smiling at me. Not the grateful smile of a child saved, no. A cruel one that raises the short hairs on the back of my neck and numb me from head to toe. His body is like that of a child, but with the wrinkled face of a hundred-year-old man, and that face is turned my way.

“I belong to you now, mistress.”

No man-child’s voice should sound as creepy as the one addressing me at the moment.

Chapter Four

"What the fuck is that?" Scrambling around, I finally manage to get on my feet, putting distance between me and the creature.

"It's a Trowe." In a few strides, Eric comes next to me, looking me up and down for any injuries. "We are not in the human realm; nothing is as it seems here. I would've told you that, but you held me back after you intercepted them."

"I did what now?" Still keeping an eye on the creature that hasn't moved an inch, I glance at Eric.

"After you pushed me away, I couldn't move from the spot. I had to force my way out of whatever hold you had over my body."

Every word he says tightens my chest and I can't prevent the panic attack that hits me out of nowhere. My breathing speeds up, cold sweat gathers on my upper lip and slides down my back. My hands tingle and numbness follows it. Dark spots dance in my vision, the ground reaching up to meet me until arms circle my body, lifting it up.

"The mistress needs time." A creepy chuckle and a voice out of my nightmares reaches my ears from behind Eric.

"Stay away from her, or I'll skin you alive," Eric snaps angrily, not taking his eyes off me. "Breathe, Hel; I won't let anything happen to you."

Staring at his face, I do just that. Concentrating on my breath, I let him hold the weight of my body until gradually, my vision clears, and my starved lungs are not hurting and screaming for oxygen. This should be a good thing. If I can hold demons back without conscious thought, that should be the best news I've heard, like ever. The fact that it's Eric is what bothers me the most, I realize. Regardless of what he is, I have no doubt in my mind that he is not evil. I may doubt many things, but that is not one of them.

Needing a distraction from my thoughts, I focus on our immediate problem.

"What's a Trowe?" Still leaning on Eric, I crane my neck to see where the creature is over his shoulders.

"Don't turn your back on it. And what does he mean I need time? It knows nothing about me."

"He won't attack, Hel. They are thieves and trouble making bastards, but he won't hurt me, or you." Turning to look at the creature, Eric's voice sounds deeper and more menacing. "Not if he knows what's good for him."

"I mean no harm, Shadow. I came to meet her as soon as the music of her blood called to me." The creepy little shit sounds closer, making my skin pebble with goose-bumps. "I only want to serve. It's been such a long time…" his words trail off, and the wistfulness in them hangs like a noose around my neck.

"Where is the ogre thingy?" Ignoring the uneasiness the creature instills in my soul, I look around for the demon that got me in this mess to start with. It's much easier to blame it on him than to admit my own stupidity caused this.

"He is not my concern." Eric dismisses my worry like we are talking about cute puppies instead of freaky demons. "They shouldn't even be here, now that you mention it." With a scowl, he looks behind him at where the creature is, I assume. "Why were the three of you here?"

The creep ignores Eric, crawling on hands and knees like a golem without his precious ring until he circles around wide enough for me to be looking at him. A shudder passes through me when he comes into view.

"He has not gone far, mistress. I can fetch him if you

wish it." Canting his head to the side, he smiles again. I'll have nightmares for a long time from that smile.

Eric frowns thoughtfully at the Trowe, not reprimanding him for anything. My mind is still a mush from everything that happened, so I just hang limply in Eric's arms gaping at the creature. From the moment I took that step off the ledge and stupidly decided going to Hell was a great idea, everything feels like a bad dream. Memories are fighting to push to the front of my mind for attention. After that damn day I found out I'm a hybrid until now, it feels like I haven't had time to stop and look at everything objectively. Michael's actions and words, my own people turning against me, and Eric coming out of nowhere to insert himself as a permanent fixture in my life. If that wasn't enough, Raphael decided to pop in and join the ride while my dead best friend came back to life and turned my team against each other. Nothing makes sense. And in the middle of it all, Eric's fairytale story of why he stayed in the human realm and his disagreement with his father, that I bought at the time because it was what I wanted to hear, is the one I focus the most on. It's the biggest bullshit of them all, I realize. Not because he was trying to lie and be deceitful, but because they all think I'm the same girl, who once upon a time believed that goodness had a name and a face.

You dumbass, you fell for it like a naïve fool. My mind decides to point out the obvious.

Looking from the creature to Eric and back, I decide at

this very moment to stop listening to everyone and start making my own mind up about everything. Eric told me when I first met him that nothing is black and white, but I'll only believe him when I see it for myself. It took a trip to Hell for the lightbulb to turn on, but at least I got there.

Narrowing my eyes on the Trowe, which only makes him smile brighter at me like he knows something I don't, I push Eric's arms away. Straightening up, the anger warms my insides when I square my shoulders. Things will never be the same again. The Holy ass let the cat out of the bag about what I am, and there is no putting it back in. I can keep fighting it, let it scratch my eyes out until I'm blind or bleed to death, or I can accept the fact that I'm an abomination not meant for Heaven or Hell and roll with it. I don't need one, or the other. The thought strikes me like one of the lightning bolts Michael loves to throw around.

They both need me.

With no idea where that leaves me, the way forward is as clear as day. There is no room for me among the righteous and pure ones, as they love to call themselves. Nor is there a room among the sinners, thanks to the empathy overriding common sense inside me. That only gives me one obvious answer. My place is in my realm beside the humans, where I can protect them from angels and demons alike, while they try to use them for whatever agendas they have. Maybe that's why my parents made me? To stand for those that don't know any better. I might be full of shit with this thought process, but it's working, and it gives me purpose. Instead of running around hiding from them all, I'm going to face them head on and show them they picked the wrong freak for their games.

"Go fetch him, golem." Addressing the creature with a toneless voice, I watch him excitedly hop a few times and ignore Eric when he stiffens next to me. Turning to face him after my dog scurries through the trees to do my bidding, I let him see my determination. "I'm a hunter. I'm going to hunt them all if they stand in my way from this day on. Be it an angel, or a demon." Eric's green eyes burn with pride I haven't seen from him before.

I'll just pray I don't let him or myself down after this proclamation.

Chapter Five

Eric

The Trowe, also known in my realm as Haltija, the one humans named gnome in their ignorance, bolted to please Helena and do what she asked. Meeting the creature changed something fundamental in her. It pains me to see that last spark of innocence get extinguished in her beautiful, expressive eyes. Inevitable it may be, but it doesn't hurt any less.

While she struggled with whatever battle she fought inside herself, I feel shame. Shame for not giving her the chance to decide for herself if she finds me worthy of her. Feeding her white lies because I think she isn't strong enough to handle the truth, which makes me a coward because the truth will come out sooner rather than later. It might bite me in the ass in the long run, but I have made my bed. I'll sleep on it now, even if it's full of thorns that will shred me to pieces. My only hope is that we both come out of this together, regardless of the trials that we will face. My shoulder blades tingle and twitch, reminding me of the wings I never thought I'd see again bursting out of my back. It can't be, but it happened. Or I am dreaming, and it's all just a figment of my imagination. I'm unwilling to test it, so I push it out of my mind.

"You have a lot of explaining to do." Not looking at me, she walks to the patch of grass near the closest trees. Pulling her dagger out, she starts wiping the blood from it, cleaning it the best she can. "The Order thought it was for my own good when they lied and manipulated me for years. I thought you were different, that *we* were different." Glancing over her shoulder, her face holds no anger or judgment. Acceptance stares at me, twisting my insides into tight knots. "I find myself standing in the middle of a storm while the anchor I thought would keep me grounded is snatched from my hands with more lies or untruths."

Watching her swipe the blade in short, practiced movements, I'm lost for what to say. She is right, of course, and I have no right to speak a word from now on unless it's the ugly, bare truth. If anything else passes my lips, I will lose her forever, mate bond or not. Coming through the portal erased the last traces of the girl I met not long ago in that alley full of rogues. Helena doesn't seem to mind, taking in stride anything life throws at her. I will mourn her loss silently in her stead. In hopes to preserve that innocent girl, I might've done damage that can't be fixed. A sharp pain stabs the center of my chest, and I promise myself right here that I will fix it. If it takes centuries, I'll fix it with each breath I take.

"I don't blame you, you know." Swiping her hair to one side, Hel smiles sadly at me. "Maybe I would've done the same if the roles were reversed. I'm not even sure what changed." Scanning the trees with an unfocused gaze, the pause she takes makes my heart thump painfully in my chest. "Actually, that's a lie. I know. There is something about that creepy thing that changed me inside." Rubbing the center of her chest with a fist, she focuses on the area where the Trowe disappeared. "Jumping to save a child, only to realize it's a thing from your nightmares, sure as hell puts things in a new perspective."

"I'm sorry, Hel." And I mean it. Inadequate as it may sound and honestly not enough, that's all I have a right to say to her.

"Meh…" Waving off my apology, she chuckles. "I honestly don't blame you. In my defense, I was in shock with it all. Maybe going to Hell personally needed to happen so I could finally snap out of it. The reality of what my life is…of what I am, hit me like a meteor. A meteor shaped like a child with an old man's face, to be precise."

"There is nothing wrong with what you are." Getting defensive on her behalf, my own anger spikes. "If anyone has a problem with that, they'll have to deal with me first."

"Always the protector." Smirking, her eyes sparkle with amusement at my outburst. "As we have come to learn, I can fight the bullies on my own, thank you very much. When I don't let anyone screw with my head, that is. That's when I learn to control this anger that keeps bubbling inside me, making me act like a child throwing a tantrum. Being reckless won't give me the chance to prove to the holy ass that he was just as wrong about me as he was right."

"The anger is the same as before we got here?" Unable to stay away from her any longer, I walk up and pull her into my arms. Pushing silky strands away from her upturned face, I search her eyes. "Is it worse now that we are in this realm?"

A line forms between her brows while she does an internal assessment, then her gaze locks on mine again. "It is slightly harder to control here. I didn't think to look at it that way until you mentioned it."

"We shouldn't mingle longer than necessary. Let's get moving so we can get out of here." Kissing her forehead, I reluctantly pull away. "We'll have time to talk about everything after we are back home."

A rustling of leaves and cracking of branches snap me around. Pushing Helena behind my back, I face whoever is tromping our way. A growl rumbles my chest when the damn Trowe jumps happily from the foliage and grins at me. Wiping the blood dribbling from his chin, he tilts his upper body sideways, craning his neck as he looks for Helena.

"Oh my God, did you eat him?" Helena comes around to stand next to me, glaring at the Trowe.

"God is not here mistress, and that God is the one that needs to kneel at your feet." The damn thing drops on his knees and crawls towards her. "The onc running away will not tell a soul about you being here. I made sure of that. I only needed the two of them to bring me to you. They outlived their usefulness as soon as you claimed me."

"Get the fuck out of here." Snapping, I lift my foot to kick him away from her. Helena surprises me by stepping between us.

"And why were you looking for me, golem?" With hands pressed on her hips, she looks down at him.

"I'm not a golem, mistress. I was tasked to guide you and protect you. I waited a long time until you needed me."

"Protect me? Did you go to the human realm, too?" Helena slides her hand behind her, gripping the dagger and watching the creature warily. "Did you kill humans while waiting on me, huh?"

"No, mistress. I've been waiting here for you. I haven't left the land in fear of missing your arrival." Looking hurt, the Trowe glances accusingly at me. "It wasn't easy to live here among the inhabitants, pretending I'm meek and defenseless, but I persevered."

"And who are you supposed to protect me from? Angels don't come down here unless they are fallen, right?" Helena looks troubled by this idea. "Who else is after my head?"

"There has been a lot of trouble, mistress. Many joined Mammon in his quest to overthrow Lucifer. They are hunting down all his allies and their children." The Trowe's mouth twists in disgust when he mentions one of the seven fallen. An Archdemon.

"Tasked to protect her by whom?" Pulling Helena away from his reach, I'm debating if she will forgive me one more thing. Like killing the Trowe after I hear what he has to say about this uproar I know nothing about.

The sprite spreads his arms like he wants to hug everything around him. The widening of his eyeless sockets makes my fists clench before he even opens his mouth to speak. "We are in the land of Wrath, Shadow. Her father tasked me before he disappeared."

Chapter Six

Helena

"You knew my father?" Hope sparks up in my chest that I will finally get some inside information about my real family. Raphael shared very little of what he knows, dropping hints here and there as it suited him. Even that seemed vague and calculated now that I think about it.

"Yessss…" The hissing sound that drones on with the raspy voice of the Trowe raises goosebumps on my arms.

Eric stands next to me, his fists clenched at his sides. If I didn't know any better, I'd think he is physically restraining himself from killing the creature. Turning my head to look at him thoroughly, I realize he actually is doing his best not to kill it. Reaching for him, I grab his forearm, hoping he can control himself. Something about the Trowe sets him on edge. Not that the creature doesn't give me the heebie jeebies, but I need to hear what it knows first.

"Well?" Glancing between the two, I prod him to continue.

"Let us not speak his name here, mistress. Even the trees have ears." Creeping up closer like it can't help itself, to my relief, his shaggy mane falls down, obscuring his face. "Lead the way, Shadow." The creature turns to Eric, and I feel his already coiled muscles stiffen more under my fingers. "You were headed in the wrong direction. She needs to see your father before all is lost."

We stand in silence. Eric's calculating, furious gaze is focused intently on the Trowe, so much I almost think he can read his mind by sheer will alone. Fear rears its head at the mention of me being anywhere near Lucifer. I shove it back with everything in me, schooling my features in a neutral mask. If I learned anything lately, it's that you should never show how you feel about things. It's a weakness that predators explore, and I'm surrounded by them, more so now than ever before in my life.

While the two of them are having a staring match, I debate my options. My life took a nose dive the moment that abomination—cringing at the word since I now use it to identify myself as well—raked its claws down my forearm, taking my blood. With everything I now know, although half of it might not be true, things look too convenient on many fronts to be a coincidence. It wasn't my first hunt, so making a rookie mistake like that, allowing any of them to get close enough to draw blood… well, it had been one of my biggest errors. What was it that pulled my focus away from my mission for that to happen?

Amanda.

My best friend's face pops in my head like a punch to the gut. She was too close to me, and I was altering my shots, so I didn't end up putting a bullet in her. We were too well oiled as a team for her to make that mistake, yet it happened. That had a snowball effect on everything, bringing me here to the depths of Hell while having a dilemma about how stupid it will be to meet Lucifer face to face.

Regardless of what I believed my whole life, the truth reared its head, shattering the glass house of lies that made my life. I don't know what to think anymore. The events of the last couple of months muddied the clear lines I had drawn of who is good and who is bad. The only thing I can rely on is my moral compass, the one I would like to think I have and is in good working order. Even that can't help much if I walk around blind, making decisions on assumptions instead of facts. Facts that only information can give me; so there is no doubt in my mind I'm not being manipulated for someone else's gain. And at the end of the day, it all comes down to that.

Intentionally or not, whoever my birth parents were, they created a weapon. Not just any weapon, no. One that can bring Heaven and Hell on their knees depending on whose hand wields it. The decision on that is obvious. The only one with the finger ready to pull the trigger will be me. And for that, I need both sides of the story. I survived the holy ass without too much damage, or so I'd like to think. Granted, Michael didn't want me dead when I was at his mercy, and he had a chance to take my life, but that's beside the point. I have to believe that Lucifer will have the same need for the special juice running through my veins. Enough to give me the opportunity to get the hell out of dodge if things turn sour. The worse that can happen is I have to fight my way out of here.

Unless I end up dead.

Locked up for as long as my extended life will last, or every drop of blood I have is drained. Refusing to dwell on the negative side of the stupidest idea I've come up with by far, I square my shoulders.

"We will go meet with your father." Since I never removed my hand from Eric's forearm, the twitching of his muscles doesn't boost my confidence about my decision.

"We will close the gate, go home to recoup, and plan. After that, we will take action." Used to being obeyed, which is evident by the way Eric believes his words are law, I almost laugh out loud. Almost.

Oh, how things have changed.

Once upon a time, I felt strongly about obeying orders, doing what I was told like the good little fool that I was. Thanks to everyone involved, I'm no longer so accommodating when being ordered what to do. The Trowe swivels his head from me to Eric, like he is watching a ping pong match. Like he doesn't want to miss even a twitch of a muscle in our exchange. Creepy!

"Okay." I'm not sure I've seen Eric look as shocked as he does at this very moment when his head snaps in my direction, flinging strands of hair over his face. "You go home handsome. The Trowe can show me the way, I'm sure." Unable to help myself, I push the hair off his forehead and tuck it behind his ear. "You go recoup, plan, and when you are ready, I'm sure you'll find me."

His lips mesh in a firm white line, amber burns and swirls in his gaze like a star ready to go supernova at the blink of an eye. My chest feels tight, but I have to do this for myself. Not because I want to hurt him or I don't value my life. It's because I do that I make my decision. With great effort, I remove my hands from him and turn to the creature that opened my eyes more than anything else so far.

"Lead the way, golem." He perks up at that, already moving in the direction we came from before I saw it. "If you are playing games or you're trying to trick me, I will enjoy killing you…very slowly."

"I only want to serve, mistress." Not even turning to look if I'll follow, he skips ahead of me. "I was tasked with guiding and protecting you. It's the greatest honor I have been granted. I will prove that I am worthy."

When my feet move and I follow the creature, I don't tell him that his idea of worthy might not be the same as mine. Life has proven me wrong on that front too. I believed I was worthy of protecting humans and being part of Heaven's army. The pure and Holy ones were deafening in their disagreement of that. So, I keep my thoughts on the matter to myself.

Almost jumping out of my skin when Eric laces his fingers through mine, I glance at him sideways. He doesn't look happy, but at least he didn't walk away and leave me behind. I'll take that as a win. Glaring at the back of the creature's head, his anger at the situation is looming like a dark cloud over both of our heads. With a squeeze of my fingers, I show him my gratitude for standing by my side even when I do idiotic things.

"Thank you," mumbling just loud enough for his ears only, my attention shifts to the sky. Hopefully no more dragons with fire wings will intercept us on our way.

"Don't thank me, Hel. I will follow you anywhere." Warmth spreads through me when his deep voice caresses my ears. "I just hoped we'd have more time before facing him."

And just like that, ice covers my insides, my heart shriveling in my ribcage. Shouldn't I be the one freaking out about meeting the Devil himself? What can be so bad that he will dread meeting his father?

Chapter Seven

The path twists and turns, leading us past the clearing with the portal where we entered this mess. Eyeing the symbols etched on the stones from afar nudges my brain like I should know what they mean or why they are there. No amount of frustration brings enlightenment on that front, so I leave that to ponder some other day. Like when I'm not walking to meet Lucifer without anyone holding me at gunpoint or forcing me to do it. The Trowe keeps skipping in front of us like a child out for a stroll, bringing in the creepy factor firmly to the front of my mind.

What the hell am I doing?

Snorting at that pun, I clear my throat when Eric looks

at me strangely. "About Mammon." Breaking the anxious silence that followed us, I keep looking around at nothing in particular. "He was one of the first fallen with Lucifer, right?"

"Yes." Anger is evident in Eric's voice. "He was one of the first seven that fell from grace."

"And what? Lucifer stole his cookies, and now they are fighting over it?" My eyes narrow when the creature slows down so it can stay within earshot of our conversation. "Keep skipping, golem. This does not concern you." Turning back to Eric, I watch his profile closely. "The question of the day is, what does any of that have to do with me? I mean, they are both in Hell, which leaves me out of the equation. They can fight as much as they want. I'll even join the cheerleading squad as long as they stay away from the human realm."

"I've stayed out of my father's business for a very long time, Hel. I know as much as you do about this." A muscle jumps in his jaw while he scans our surroundings, as if expecting an attack at any moment. "Maddison is the one keeping tabs on the comings and goings around here. She never mentioned anything." Finally, he turns my way so I face him as well. "I would think something like this is important enough to garner her attention, as well as mine. My cousin will have some explaining to do when we go back, I assure you." Judging by the look on his face, I wouldn't want to be Maddison when we see her. "As far as what you have to do with it? Your guess is as good as mine. But, since they involved you, I'm making it my business now. Maybe staying out of things was not such a great move on my part. I'll remedy that."

"I should've paid closer attention during bible studies. It just didn't seem important to know the names and powers of what you think are made up characters, especially when all you know for sure is that rogues exist. All I was interested in was becoming a hunter and sending abominations back to Hell. I didn't care if they had names." Pressing a couple fingers to my temple, I start massaging it to relieve some of the pressure of the building headache. "Hindsight, huh?"

"It's not your fault they kept you ignorant. It's easier to manipulate someone when they aren't aware of the truth." Understanding how that sounded, he winces without me saying a word. "And what a hypocrite I turned out to be."

"You like to keep me ignorant so that you can manipulate me, as well?" My words are soft, but the creature hears them, nonetheless. Hissing like a rabid animal, it turns towards Eric, baring its yellowed teeth. "Hold your horses, golem. I'm a big girl; I can take punches as good as I can give them." Glancing at Eric, I swallow the lump trying to lodge itself in my throat. "Even the emotional ones."

"Helena…" Stopping in his tracks, Eric grabs both my hands in his. He is holding me so tight that I can feel the bones grinding, which makes my stomach drop to my feet.

Bracing myself, I'm too afraid of what he is about to say, so I focus on his Adam's apple, unable to meet his eyes. "I might have embellished the truth and told you a watered-down version of my reasons for staying away from my realm. I did it out of selfish reasons because I didn't want you to see me for the monster I am. Not to manipulate you." Lifting my face with a crooked finger under my chin, he forces me to lock gazes with him. "Never to manipulate or use you for your blood or for who and what you are."

I want to believe him with everything in me, but experience holds me back. His face becomes blurry when unshed tears flood my eyes. Blinking them away, I give him a rope. He can use it to pull himself out of the mess he made, or he can use it as a noose. I can't give him more than that at the moment.

"I won't trust words, Eric. It's those that have led me almost to lose my life. Words allowed those I held dear to betray me. I'll trust actions from now on. That's all I can give you right now."

"That's all I'm asking, and it's more than I deserve." His eyes soften, the emerald green bleeding through the amber. "Thank you." His lips press to mine, halting any thought that would've pushed its way up.

Wrapping my arms around his shoulders, spearing my fingers through his hair, I hold him close while his tongue twines with mine. Butterflies erupt in my lower belly when Eric yanks me flush to his body, his hand grabbing a handful of my ass. His hardness presses on my stomach, and my fingers claw his skin to bring him even closer to me. A tortured groan rips from his throat, spurring me on. His touch, his taste, is all I know, and it makes me forget where we are and what waits for us here. Feeling like somebody is watching clears the fog in my head enough for me to pull my mouth away from Eric's. He continues to place open-mouthed kisses and nips on my jaw and neck while my unfocused eyes look around us. When my gaze lands on a wrinkled face with blackened eye sockets too close to us for comfort, a scream is torn from my lips. Eric flips me behind his back, searching for the threat.

"Your father will be pleased, mistress." The Trowe watches us with a too-broad smile, splitting his ugly face within arm's reach.

"He scared the shit out of me." Panting, I gasp for air with my forehead to Eric's back, doing my best to keep my heart within my ribcage with my hands on my chest. "I forgot he was there."

"Go keep watch." Growling, Eric kicks the creature, lifting him a few inches off the ground, sending him flying in the hedge on the side of the path. A yelp is all that's heard from the Trowe before he dives headfirst in the bushes.

"Don't hurt him." I have no idea why I'm worried about the stupid thing, but he is growing on me for some reason.

"He'll be fine." Scolding when the Trowe pops his

head up, Eric pulls me back in his arms. "He is lucky I didn't rip his head off."

"The mistress won't like that, Shadow." Crawling out like vermin, the creature gloats but stays out of reach. Maybe he is not as stupid as I thought. A snort makes me slap a hand over my mouth at the expression on Eric's face.

To defuse the tension, I pull Eric's attention to me. "Yes, Shadow, the mistress won't like that one bit." His eyebrow lifts up, making me laugh. "I think I'll get you to start calling me mistress, too." My belly clenches at the hunger in his eyes. "It might give a new perspective on things."

He opens his mouth, anticipation making me giddy to hear what he will say, but the Trowe kills my joy. I need to get used to that with the creature around.

"We have company," he hisses, diving for the bushes again.

Eric pulls me in the cover of the trees before the hissing echo of the Trowe's words has finished drifting in the air.

Chapter Eight

I guess Eric doesn't want to leave things to chance after my display of obedience, or lack thereof, the last time we were in this situation. Instead of taking the tree next to me for cover, he has me sandwiched between his body and the wide tree trunk. My girly bits didn't get the memo about the danger lurking, so they get excited by his nearness. Reigning in my hormones, I almost swallow my tongue when the Trowe squeezes his tiny ass between us.

"What the hell are you doing?" whisper-yelling, I nudge him away from me with my hipbone.

The lines pull down around his mouth when he turns his face up to look at me. Can he look at me if he has holes where his eyes should be? Shaking my head to clear it and disperse the silly thoughts that I use to keep myself from freaking out at moments like this, I strain my ears to hear what got the creature worked up. I wish I had as good of hearing as Eric. Although, I'm much better than an average human, his is still superior to mine.

The anger that's been quiet giving me the reprieve I needed pushes to the surface. Mentally sinking claws in it, I push it down where it belongs. Like he can read my mind, the concern is all over Eric's face when he looks down at me. With a slight jerk of my head, I tell him that he shouldn't be worried, at least not yet.

Deep, gravelly voices float up to where we are standing motionless in the cover of the surrounding forest. The shuffling of feet and thumps of many boots on the ground become louder the closer they are to us. Eric's chest vibrates under my palm when the Trowe wraps an arm around me and hangs sideways to watch the path like a monkey. This whole thing is so messed up that my body shakes with the laughter I'm suppressing so I don't give our location away.

"We will stay here to see if they show up on this side." The first words, clear enough to be heard, sound like they are coming from two rocks grinding together.

"It will help to climb the ranks if it's us bringing the heir to Mammon." Chuckling that almost makes my ears bleed is followed by a grunt. "Keep your hands to yourself before I rip your arm off and beat you with it." I guess he got punched for his chuckling.

Glancing up at Eric, I see him watching me closely. His head is tilted slightly to the side and uneasiness crawls up my spine. The expression on his face is one he gets when he is considering something he never thought of before. If he is worried that they are looking for him, considering their mention of an heir, he doesn't show it. The group of demons is passing us now, so I ignore the icy fingers inching up my vertebrae. By the sound of it, there are at least a dozen of them walking in a group. They must be headed to the clearing of the portal to wait for us to fall into their hands. Too bad for them enough time has passed, my poor tailbone even stopped throbbing from landing there hours ago. They can sit and wait as long as they like. Relaxing my stiff body, I lean back and let the tree carry my weight.

The Trowe turns his head to check on me before continuing his watch over the progression. I can still feel Eric's intense focus on me, but I ignore him. Closing my eyes, only the sound of feet getting further away from us has my attention. I didn't need to see the demons to know they looked exactly like the two ogre dudes that were manhandling my creature. *What the hell? Since when did I start calling the Trowe my anything?*

Snapping my eyes open, I get snarled in Eric's gaze like a fly in a spiderweb.

Thankfully no sound can be heard for a few long

moments. I push him away from me, and he takes a step back without arguing about it. Narrowing my eyes suspiciously at him for complying, I watch him for a second before untangling the Trowe from my waist and shoving him away, as well.

"Whatever you are thinking, keep it to yourself." Pitching my voice as low as possible, I glare at him. "I have enough shit to sort through at the moment. I don't need more of it."

His lips twitch, but he gives me a sharp nod. That makes me warier of whatever it is that's going through his head. The Trowe decides to jump on the path, saving me from overthinking everything. Pushing my way behind him, I look both ways before stepping out in the open. Not waiting on us, the creature starts walking fast in the direction we are headed, like his ass is on fire. Unwilling to lose sight of him, I hurry down the path. A yelp I'm familiar with by now thanks to Eric playing soccer with the creature earlier is the only warning I get before I turn the bend in the path. I almost slam my face into Eric's chest.

"What the fuck is wrong with you?" Taking a deep breath to stop the galloping happening in my chest, I slam my fists on my hips. "You almost gave me a heart attack."

"Did I now?" Tilting his head to the side, a smile stretches his lips.

"Let him go." Pointing my chin towards the dangling Trowe he holds off the ground by the neck, my anger bubbles up so fast I have no time to push it down. "I told you not to hurt him. Don't be an asshole!" The ground under my feet starts trembling slightly, making me sway.

"Well, I'll be damned," Eric drawls, his grin stretching his lips wide while he is looking at me like a teenage boy that discovered Playboy magazine for the first time.

"There is something seriously wrong with you, monster boy!" Watching him warily, I take a step away from him. Something is not right. Alarms start blaring in my head while the Trowe flails, doing his best to free himself from Eric's grip.

My breathing speeds up the longer I watch the man in front of me. All sorts of wrong vibes crawl over my skin while he looks me up and down. Even when I first saw Eric, I've never felt disgusted or dirty when those green eyes mapped every curve or dip on my body. I feel all of that this very moment as I take another step back and I bounce off a firm chest behind me. Arms wrap protectively around me, one over my chest and the other circling my waist. With dread filling every inch of me, I slowly turn my head and look over my shoulder.

Eric has me in the safety of his arms, glaring daggers at whoever it is that I just met. My trembling hand slides between us, grabbing the hilt of the blade I keep in the small of my back. When I look in front of me, I blink a few times in hopes I'll see something different. Nothing changes, and Eric is standing in front of me as well. Only he is wearing a shirt I didn't notice the first time.

"Release the Haltija," Eric, from behind me, says without inflection in his voice.

"As you wish." Eric in front of me smirks, dropping the Trowe like a rock not taking his eyes off of me. "I didn't expect to see you back so soon." He finally lifts his gaze and looks at the man behind me. "To what do we owe this pleasure?" Glancing at me, his smirk grows "Don't answer that. I can see the appeal."

"I'm not in the mood for playing games, Colt. What the fuck is going on here?" Eric growls, tightening his arms around me. My mind short-circuits when he gives the other Eric a name.

"Very well, have it your way. You were never a fun person to have around, anyway." Chuckling, he looks at me again. "The name is Colt, as you already know now, sweetheart. We can discuss things when we get out of the open." Turning around, he starts walking away from us. I just stand there, leaning back against Eric, who is gaping like a carp left too long out of water.

"Eric?" Sounding breathless, I do my best to swallow through a dry throat.

It's not Eric that answers me. Colt looks over his shoulder, first winking at me, then grinning at Eric. "Good to see you back home, brother."

Damn it! There are two of them! Like one was not hard enough to deal with.

Chapter Nine

Eric

"What are you doing here?" Tucking a still stunned Helena under my arm, I put myself between her and my brother.

"Father sent me to check in case you decided to come to your senses." Subtle, Colt is not. He keeps glancing at my mate, making my fist itch to meet his face. "I thought he was getting desperate and grasping at straws. The joke is on me."

"I have no intention of staying." Making it clear there is no more discussion on the matter, I switch gears. "He sent you alone to check a portal gate? He knows what's going on in the human realm, does he not? Michael is going out of his mind to be able to get his hands on any of us." The smile on his face slips for a split second, but he recovers quickly. Too bad I know him as well as I know myself. "Don't tell me. He got tired of your bullshit and figured it's the best way to get rid of you."

"Or I decided it's better to call it quits than clean up the shit storm you left behind." Nonchalantly, he throws the jab. "What's with the Haltija?" Pointing his chin at the creature skipping alongside us, Colt cuts off my retort.

"It attached itself to Helena." I feel her stiffen next to me, so I rub my hand up and down her arm. "It's proving useful, for now."

"I should've guessed." Musing, my brother turns to Helena. "The entire realm is looking for you, sweetheart. Lucky for you, I found you first."

"Holy shit, there are two of you." Helena turns her wide green eyes on me, stopping me from removing Colt's head off his shoulders. I guess the shock wore off.

"I'm sorry I didn't tell you." At her narrowed gaze, I pull her closer to me. "I never thought I'd see him again. And you,"—Turning to my brother, I pronounce every word clearly, so there is no mistake—"found nothing first. We were coming to see father."

"You mean you hoped you'd never see me again," Colt points out. "And if you are letting her walk around wherever she wants on her own, I don't think you are fit to keep an eye on her."

"Letting me?" the way Helena says that, with the sweetest tone I've heard, makes me grin at Colt. He walked into this one all on his own, and I'll enjoy every second of it. "Letting me? I heard you correctly, right?"

"He should've brought you to father the moment you stepped foot here. I'm sure he will find better protection for you." My brother lodges the foot he put in his mouth firmly with each word. My grin grows.

"Because I need to be told what I can and cannot do. And where I can or cannot go, right?" The innocence on her face contradicts the fury burning in her gaze.

Oblivious to my mates temper, Colt keeps digging his grave. "Of course. You shouldn't be running around unchecked here. Anyone can snatch you, and we are all screwed if that happens. If it was up to me, I'd lock you up where no one could find you. You'd, be safe, then." Nodding at her encouragingly, he even smiles.

Removing my arm from around her, Helena stops me with a hand on my chest. I let her walk up to my brother, who gloats, probably thinking she is going to him to keep her safe. Lifting an arm when she is close enough to tuck her under it, as I had done before, is the only thing she gives him time for.

Fast as lightning, Helena's fist connects first with his ribs, the crunching sound like music to my ears, before it flies up, catching him under his jaw. The force of the punch flings his head back, taking his body with him. Colt's body hits the ground, dust puffing up around him like a cloud. My mate walks up to him, pressing her boot on his throat. His eyes bulge, and his stunned face is something I'll never forget as long as I live.

"How about now, jerk?" She grinds the heel of her boot, making him choke and grab her ankle to release the pressure. "You wanna lock me up now?"

Unable to stop myself, I start laughing. The Trowe circles Colt, giggling like a deranged child. It makes me laugh harder. Pushing him away with her foot, she turns to look at me.

"Can we get this over with and get out of here? I'm pretty sure that it's frowned upon if I start killing your family members this early in our relationship."

"Relationship?" Colt chokes, lifting on his elbows. My laughter dies a sudden death, dread replacing it.

"Let's get out of here; we can talk later." Striding forward, I grab Helena's hand and pull her along with me. "You said yourself it's not safe to linger here, no matter how entertaining it is to see her beat your ass."

Both my mate and my brother watch me with suspicion, but luckily none of them say anything as we move at a fast pace towards my father's palace. The tops of the towers can finally be seen through the trees. That's enough to take Helena's attention, allowing me to glance at my brother. Colt hasn't taken his eyes off me, so I make sure he sees on my face that he better keeps his mouth shut. Especially about things that don't concern him.

The Trowe looks between us, his wrinkled face

flicking left and right while he mumbles something unintelligible under his breath. If I'm not mistaken, he says something along the line of eating the face of whoever causes his mistress grief, but I can't be sure.

"Is that where we are going?" I can hear her swallow thickly before she turns to me.

"Yes, we should be there within the hour." I can't blame her for feeling anxious about meeting my father. He is an imposing presence, even to his own children, at least if Colt and I are anything to go by.

As luck would have it, no more words are spoken, and no one crosses our paths all the way to the gates. Helena doesn't let go of my hand, even when she knows I can feel her cold, sweaty palm and the twitching of her fingers. The fates help us all in the next few hours. We will either find the answers we need, or this will break me, releasing the beast I've kept in check for so long. If that happens, Mammon will not be the biggest threat the realms have seen.

With that in mind, and ignoring my brother's poking stare between my shoulder blades, I push the gates of the place I haven't called home for lifetimes open.

Chapter Ten

Helena

I hesitate at the open gates, halting Eric's movement. He looks back at me but doesn't push me one way or another. I almost believe that he has learned his lesson about not making decisions on my behalf. Maybe putting Colt on his ass was motivation enough to get him started. I guess a girl needs to throw a few punches around to be taken seriously. Shooting him a couple of times didn't do the trick so well.

Something is bothering him, as well, to the point that he is willing to control himself. If I start thinking about what that may be, I'll go insane, so I just go with the flow.

Whatever it is, it's not like I can change it. When the time comes, I'll deal with it, or not. It depends on how bad it is.

"Why are we standing here?" Colt comes to situate himself next to my shoulder, looking from Eric to me and back.

I keep my gaze locked on Eric's. When I cross this threshold, I understand the little grasp of normality I've held onto will be lost to me forever. With certainty I haven't felt about anything else before now, I know that my world is about to shift on its axis. Am I ready for it?

Hell no, I'm not ready.

Do I have a choice in the matter? If I want to stop being the blind sheep among the pack of hungry wolves, the answer is simple. No, I don't have a choice. Anchoring myself in Eric's calm and resigned gaze, I slowly walk through the threshold.

It's…uneventful.

Disappointment hits me when nothing happens now that I'm standing inside Lucifer's home. Not that I was expecting him to jump from the shadows and try to bite my head off or anything. I just thought it'd make me feel different.

"You okay?" Eric comes closer, and as always, his main concern is that I'm okay before anything else. I miss the asshole he used to be sometimes.

"Peachy." The strained smile I offer him doesn't convince him on the truthfulness of my words. "I'm fine, really." Uncomfortable under his prodding perusal, I look at the open doors for the first time.

With lips parted in wonder, my fingers lift and trace the beautiful scenes depicted in what looks like etched, black glass. Angels and demons in the middle of battles have been carved in all their beautifully horrific glory. Their faces cut in sharp, determined lines, wings spread wide, or horns pushed forward. I can feel their pain, determination, and their hunger for victory, which is so intense that it takes my breath away. As my fingers glide over it, warmth spreads through my hand. Red pulsing light comes from the door, getting brighter the longer I hold my skin pressed on it. The ground under my feet trembles, forcing me to place my entire palm on the glass so I can stay standing.

"What in the fates is that?" Colt growls from somewhere, but I can't pull my gaze away from the pulsing light.

"Hel…" Whatever Eric was about to say gets lost in the whooshing air that flings my hair over my face, blocking the light and the door from view.

With a loud gasp, I snap out of the trance that pulled me under as soon as I touched the door. "I need to get out of here." Grabbing Eric's hand, I'm ready to bolt out of the place, but when I turn, Colt is blocking my exit." Get the hell out of my way."

"I'm afraid I can't do that, sweetheart." Smirking, he folds his arms over his chest.

"You can. I just need to help you move."

I only manage one step towards him when the doors start swinging closed. My eyes widen when Colt throws his body at me, and I have no time to brace for the impact. He slams into me like a battering ram, and with an *oomph*, my back hits Eric's chest since he was right behind me. All three of us end up sprawled in a tangled mess of limbs, with only the Trowe standing above us. He is watching with interest, while the last silvery glow of the moon fades over his ugly face.

There is a horrible finality in the thudding sound when the doors close, pitching us in darkness. We all lay frozen for a moment before Eric starts spitting insults at his brother, pushing him off me. The incredulity of this whole thing makes me giggle. The giggle turns into a burst of hysterical laughter that echoes around us eerily.

"Hel." Shoving Colt further away from me, Eric pushes the hair out of my face. I can't see him, but I can feel his worried gaze on me. "What's wrong? Talk to me."

"The land can be overwhelming at times if you are not used to it," a new voice says from somewhere above my head.

The simple words are spoken with a lilting accent, making them sound sophisticated. Whoever it is, they can be reading a dinner menu, and no sane person will be able to resist a sigh, the same one that passes through my lips. My entire body turns into a limp noodle, melting into a puddle on the hard floor.

Eric stiffens, a horrific growl coming out of him like a dog guarding a bone.

"Shhhh…" My hand slaps all over his face before I find his mouth and hold it closed. "Let him speak."

Prying my fingers off his face, Eric huffs and lifts up, pulling me along with him. A masculine chuckle bounces off the walls, giving the illusion that we are in a cave underground. A memory nudges my brain like I've heard it before, but I can't put my finger on it. Blinking in the darkness doesn't help at all. Not knowing what frcsh hell is about to hit us, now that my brain is out of the gutter thanks to not having Eric's half-naked body all over me, I keep them closed and concentrate on sound.

"Enough with the theatrics." Pulling me closer to him, Eric snaps at whoever is here with us. "She won't appreciate it, I assure you."

"What are you talking about?" My question ends with an embarrassing yelp when a tiny hand grabs mine before I remember the damn Trowe. "Stop touching me." Snatching my hand away, I press closer to Eric. "That will get you stabbed really fast."

"Apologies." The beautiful voice floats in the darkness, full of amusement, a moment before candles burst to life all around us.

The wander of the orangey glow, casting everything in an almost romantic light, fades in a split second when my eyes land on the man facing us. He is in the middle of a long hallway, his hands pushed in the pockets of pressed, elegant pants, watching me with rapt interest. A black dress shirt with the top two buttons open stretches over his broad chest and tucks in the pants at his narrow waist. He is a sight to behold, as alluring as all the stories make him out to be, and then some. My mouth dries up, preventing me from swallowing the lump the size of Atlanta that is stuck in my throat. There is no mistaking who came to welcome us into his domain. If the power rolling off of him in waves didn't give him away, the too beautiful face, more sinful than anyone's face has a right to be, would've.

"Welcome, Helena." His lips pull on one side in an almost smile while I gape at him stupidly. "These are unpredictable times, I'm afraid. You will have to forgive me for wanting to confirm who you really are before I allow you entrance."

"The door." Balling my fists, I let my anger come to the surface, clearing the fuzz in my brain. The asshole was messing with my head on purpose.

Inclining his head regally, like I'm a puppy that learned a new trick, he keeps watching me. The floor under my feet starts shaking violently, but he doesn't bat an eye. His smile keeps growing, pissing me off even more.

"Lucifer." Squeezing the name through clenched teeth and glaring at him, I lift my chin defiantly. "Your buddy Michael didn't manage to intimidate me by throwing his powers around. Neither will you."

I'm grateful Eric stays out of it, allowing me to show

this jerk that I'm not a scared little girl they can all push around. It might help him get my forgiveness for being an ass and not telling me the truth. Lucifer throws his head back, his black hair brushing his shoulders. The allure of his laughter makes my skin pebble.

"Come." After he is done laughing at me, he turns and starts walking further into the never-ending hallway. "We need to talk."

Chapter Eleven

"Like shit was not weird enough, your father has to look like he is your age, huh?" spitting the words angrily at Eric, I stomp after Lucifer. Like that's the most important thing. Ignoring the fact that first Colt, and now Lucifer, knew my name before anyone mentioned it gets shoved in the back of my head for later.

Eric doesn't answer, only lifts an eyebrow at me. We continue down the hallway with the Trowe taking point and Colt bringing up the rear. If I didn't know better, I'd think he was a security measure in case we decide to bolt for the doors. Glancing over my shoulder at the said doors, a shiver passes through me. I hope there is another exit from this place.

Stumbling slightly, I frown at the floor. The smooth mirror-like surface is cracked at uneven intervals like a mega-earthquake has hit the place and split it open. The cracks are no wider than an inch or two, not enough for us to drop through it—a fact I'm more than grateful for. Tiny flames flicker like someone has placed tea candles to mask the scarred floor. The deeper we go; the more silly things seem. With only fires for light, it feels like we are walking through a night sky. The faint scent of musk drifts through the air.

"Look, mistress." The creepy voice of the creature yanks me from the magic this place is using to mess with my brain. He is pointing excitedly at the fork in the hallway, the direction I saw Lucifer's back disappear a second ago. When we reach it, my feet falter, but Eric doesn't let Colt see my hesitation. Tugging me along, he steers us through this new twist in Lucifer's labyrinth.

Clocks.

Hundreds of clocks in various shapes and sizes cover both sides of the walls. As we pass them, I notice none of them are working. They are stopped, all of them at the same time. No matter where I look, six o'clock stares at me from each mechanical face. Glancing at Eric, I see him flicking his eyes, checking the damn clocks as well. His gaze narrows, and I can almost hear his teeth grinding. Squeezing his fingers, I shake my head subtly to stop whatever he is planning on doing. His nostrils flare, but he gives me a barely perceptible jerk of his head. We need to hear what Lucifer has to say and get out of here.

If we get out of here.

The gloomy thought is like a knife through me. So, just like everything else, I leave it for later if there is a need for it. I'm sure if they wanted me dead, they would've acted differently. Maybe they're trying to get me to cooperate without being forced. Whatever their agenda is, I'll have to act as a willing participant until I'm out of here.

Everything will be fine, I tell myself sternly.

I need information and Lucifer has it. I'm not foolish enough to think he will give me what I want without getting something in return. Whether I'm willing to pay the price or not, that's left to be determined.

"We are almost there," Eric says softly next to me.

As if his words conjure it, the end of the hallway appears. Double doors, wide and tall enough to fit a tank, wait for us, partly open. The slit between them looks wide enough for us to walk through, one by one. Uneasiness claws at me, but I stiffen my shoulders.

Don't show weakness. With that mantra in my head, ignoring the cold sweat sliding down my back, I keep moving. The flickering of light through the cracked open doors tells me there is more candlelight in that room, as well.

Eric guides me with a warm palm pressed at the small of my back, unaware of the turmoil in me. He looks pissed, but not worried. That's a good thing, right? When his fingers catch on the dagger I have tucked in my waistband, I stiffen, almost stopping in my tracks. Guilt stabs me when he only adjusts his hand, ignoring it. I'm getting paranoid the longer I am in this castle of doom. Before we walk through the doors, it hits me why I'm creeped out so much. This hallway is as silent as the one leading to Maddison's office. The silence is so oppressive that it's enough to drive you insane.

The Trowe waits for us at the doors like he can feel my trepidation. In a way, I'm grateful for the gesture, regardless of how much he freaks me out.

"Come in," Lucifer calls from inside the room. "Time is wasting."

"Does time matter to you?" Steeling my spine, I strut inside like I own the place. "Looking at your collection out there," I start, itching a thumb over my shoulder and staring at his back, "I would think you couldn't care less."

"So reckless." Chuckling, he looks over his shoulder. "Sit."

Since it's not a request but a command, I bristle. Eric, knowing me too well, grabs me by the elbow and drags me closer to his father, plopping me on soft cushions. When my ass sinks in softness I've never felt before, I finally look around. The room is wide with high ceilings. Bookshelves line the walls, stacked to bursting with leather bounds and scrolls. Four sofas are placed in a half-circle in front of the most prominent fireplace I've ever seen, one chair fit for a king nestled between them. Lucifer is standing with his back to us, staring at the roaring flames. Opening my mouth to start pissing him off more, the words get stuck in my throat when my eyes flick above the mantle. Black wings with greenish-silvery tips that shimmer like a rainbow are stretched above the fire, framed in glass. Something about them brings tears to my eyes, but I blink them away. All the anger drains from me, and I clear my throat, twice, before I can speak.

"You knew who I was before I even told you my name." I can't hide the accusation in my voice.

Turning around slowly, Lucifer keeps his accessing gaze on me for a long time before turning to Eric. After he pushed me on the sofa, Eric didn't sit, but he also didn't move even an inch away from me. Looming above me, he stares at his father with his arms crossed over his bare chest. Colt stays leaning on the doors we used to walk in, and the Trowe roams around the room, sniffing everything within reach.

"I would say it is nice to see you, but I can tell it's not mutual." Lucifer smiles sadly at his son.

"You wouldn't be wrong." Obviously, in Hell, Eric is a man with very little words.

"I have Helena to thank for finally seeing my son in over a century." Inclining his head at me, I almost jump up to curtsy like an idiot. The fallen angel sure knows how to affect people.

"This is not a family reunion," Eric snaps. "What in

the fates is going on, and how did Abaddon manage to get past the wards in the portal to the human realm so soon after a hunter sent him back?"

"With a bullet between his eyes," I quip when he is done, in case we are taking records of how the demon died. Eric squeezes the bridge of his nose with a thumb and forefinger, so I glare at the side of his head.

"I am to assume it was your doing?" Cocking his head like a bird, Lucifer's black eyes twinkle, and what looks like quicksilver passes through them a few times.

"You are avoiding my question," Eric growls.

"Mammon has gone insane." Waving an elegant hand with long fingers, Lucifer wrinkles his nose, twisting his lips like he smells something bad. "I have let him do what he pleases for far too long. Like spoiled children, they are throwing a tantrum, thinking if they take my place they can do what they want."

"Can they?" I wince internally when his eyes lock on mine again. I should learn to keep my mouth shut. "Take your place I mean."

"What do you think, girl? Have I ruled this realm since the beginning because anyone can take it from me?"

"Oh, wow. Breathe dude. I didn't mean to insult you; I'm just asking. Until a couple of months ago, I thought they made you up." My eyebrows hit my hairline, pure innocence plastered on my face.

"Did she just call me dude?" Lucifer looks from Eric to Colt with what I think is shock on his face. Bracing myself for him to go ape-shit, my jaw hits the floor when a deep belly laugh shakes his body. "You are so much like your father." Slapping a hand on his thigh, he keeps laughing.

"My…" Blinking fast, I try to unlock my jaw and untangle my tongue. "You knew my father?"

"Knew?" All laughter dies down, and he frowns at me. "I KNOW your father. I don't know how Mammon managed to trap him. I have no doubt Satanael is well and will find a way out."

All air gets sucked out of the room, and everything around me fades to blessed darkness.

Chapter Twelve

Eric

"Satanael's daughter." After making sure Helena is as comfortable as she can be, I turn to my father. "I don't know why I didn't connect the dots when Raphael talked about her parents."

"Raphael?" Leaning an elbow on the hand rest of his chair, he places one ankle over his knee, smoothing his pant-leg thoughtfully. "He has an interest in the girl I take it?"

"Everyone has an interest in her, thanks to that bastard Abaddon." Pushing the words through clenched teeth, I scowl at my fists. "I will skin him alive when I get my hands on him. It'll take him a few centuries to regrow all the parts I will rip apart with my bare hands."

"You fought tooth and nail for this not to be your problem." My father's words feel like hot oil poured over my insides. "You renounced your title and your place by my side to make sure this will never be your problem." The silence is pressing the weight of the worlds on top of my chest. "What changed?"

Knuckles white, I relish the pain when my claws burst and sink into my palms. A muscle ticks in my jaw, the sound of my grinding teeth too loud to my ears. Saying nothing, I keep glaring at my fists. The fates have played the biggest joke of the millennia on me.

"Colt?" I flick my gaze to him when he addresses my twin brother.

"Yes, father?" Always the obedient one, he snaps to attention. I glare at him for that.

"Leave us!"

Colt's face turns red in fury. Nostrils flaring, he opens his mouth, thinks better of it, and storms out of the room, slamming the doors behind him. As petty as it may be, I smirk at the closed entrance.

"Well?" With a narrowed gaze, he prompts me.

"What do you want me to say?" Pushing off the sofa so I don't wake Helena, I start pacing in front of the fireplace.

"How about answering my question." Lifting a hand

palm up, and wordlessly calling me an idiot, he waits patiently.

"I am not you." Whirling on him, I get in his face. "I will never be you, and I will never play these mind games all of you enjoy." Flinging a hand at Helena, I make sure he understands me without a shadow of a doubt. "And neither will she. I will bet my soul on it. You and Santanael have another think coming if you think you will make her do anything she doesn't want to do."

"Boy, you have already lost much on your bets." His gaze lands over my shoulder above the mantle. It's like a physical punch to the chest. "Soon you will have nothing left to bargain with if you keep it up."

"She is my mate!" roaring in his face, my body shakes with the force of holding back and not punching his smug face. "I will give all I am willingly to protect her from your schemes."

"That cannot be!" Lifting to his full height, his face darkens with anger. "You gave up that right and swore off her when you turned your back on me." His power slams into me, hitting me square in the chest and lifting me off my feet. My body hits the wall, and the sound of bones breaking is accompanied by excruciating pain. "Colt took your place. I will sever your bond, and you'll have your wish. You will be free to roam the human realm."

Fear and anger push me up. Swaying on my feet, I face him. The pity in his eyes rips my heart to shreds. With an anguished roar, I tackle him. He will have to kill me before he takes her away from me. Our tangled limbs hit his chair, breaking it to pieces. Splinters pierce my skin, rearranging broken ribs and bones. He flings me off him like a piece of lint, straightening up. With determination set on his face, darkness swirls around his fingertips like tendrils of a Kraken ready to devour my essence. Only him or an Archangel can destroy the soul of an immortal.

And my father is about to destroy mine.

I wish I had told Helena that she owns my soul. Even destroyed, it'll belong to her, no matter where it ends up. Regrets that I never told her the truth will haunt me even when I'm irrevocably gone. She deserves better. Maybe Colt will do better than I ever could. As the tendrils grow on his hands, my eyes search for my mate. I want her face to be the last I see before I am no more. The brawl has pushed everything around, and I can't even see a lock of her hair from where I'm sprawled on the floor. Closing my eyes, I recall her smiling face and brace for the pain that will come. Holding my breath, I wait.

And I wait…

When an eternity passes, and I still feel every broken bone in my body, I crack my eyelids open. My father is still standing where he was, his face twisted in a mask of anger I've rarely seen on him. His arms are lifted to the sides, palm up, but no tendrils swirl around them. No darkness crawls toward me, ready to devour my soul.

The pain must be messing with my head because he

looks like he has grown another set of arms. No, wait! It's legs. What in the fates? Blinking fast, I try to clear my vision, but the legs are still there. Scanning the rest of his body, my eyes widen when I see a familiar dagger pressed under his chin. The damn Trowe is also clinging to his leg, baring his teeth and hissing.

"Are you planning to take a nap first or are you going to get your ass up, monster boy?" Helena pokes her head out from behind my father.

With a groan, I lift myself up. She is wrapped around my father piggyback style, her steady hand pressing the dagger to his jugular. While his eyes swirl with silver, he hasn't moved or tried to dislodge her. Bracing on the closest sofa, I finally stand up on my feet.

"Don't hurt her." Stumbling a step, I reach for her. "Do what you will with me but leave her be. She thinks she is helping me."

"I am helping you, asshole." Scolding me from behind his shoulder, she presses the dagger harder. "We learned that sharp pointy things can even cut through the mighty Lucifer, just like a knife through butter." With her free hand, she slaps him none too gently on his face, shocking me stupefied. "Didn't we?" she asks sweetly.

"I might've misjudged the situation." His words make me blink once. Maybe I am dead. "Let us all calm down and discuss this."

"A few drops of blood and everyone wants to calm

down and talk." Snickering, Helena lifts her eyebrows in question. "Should I remove the dagger?"

Reaching for her again, I nod once. "Come to me, Hel."

Jumping off him, she backs away slowly until I pull her in my arms. To my delight as bad as it may be, she places herself protectively in front of me, the dagger swirling with power in her hand. The symbols blink like a light show, one after another, in a mesmerizing display. I catch my father watching it with interest, too.

"Helena, I think I need to explain." Regardless of what happens, I don't want her harmed if I'm not around to protect her.

"No need, I heard." She doesn't look away from the target of her anger.

"All of it?" My gut tightens.

"Enough of it to call bullshit." Pointing the dagger at my father's chest, her voice gives me chills. "No one severs any bonds if they value their lives. You might be powerful enough to kill me Lucifer, but I will take as many of you as I can before I die."

Chapter Thirteen

Helena

Hearing that you are a hybrid, born from a demon and an angel that got their rocks off, is one thing. Understanding that you are the actual Devil's spawn is entirely different. I'm not feeling particularly proud of fainting when I was told my father is Satanael.

Or, Satan, if you will.

When the name passed Lucifer's lips, the first thought that hit me was: *Eric and I are related, and I slept with him.* It was followed up by the confusion of Lucifer talking about himself like he is two different people. Well, entities if you want to be specific. All that happened from one breath to the next, turning the lights out for me.

I consider it lucky that it only lasted no longer than a minute. Coming around just in time to overhear part of their conversation would've been enlightening if I knew what the hell they were talking about. Sticking to my decision to make my own mind up on things, I used Lucifer's distraction when he tried to kill Eric to my advantage. Even now, he is still watching me like I've grown another head for sneaking up on him, close enough to leave a thin slice on his neck.

The dagger in my hand sends a pulse of energy through my arm. It got animated after feeling Lucifer's blood on its blade. I'm just adding it to the creepy factor of this road trip I'm taking through Hell.

"Shall we…"

"We shall not," cutting off Lucifer, I wave the dagger in his face, not moving away from Eric. "It's obvious you don't want me dead, or I wouldn't be standing here now. That being said, let's get a few things clear." Leaning forward, I lift both eyebrows mockingly. "You are not my father."

Now I feel like a nerd making Star Wars references while Lucifer jerks back as if I've slapped him. Shrugging a shoulder, ignoring the fact that Eric's arms go slack around me, I don't look away.

"I never implied that you were my daughter."

Speaking slowly with a confused expression, Lucifer is scrutinizing me like he wants to judge my sanity.

"You said my father is Satan, okay, Satanael." Maybe I should've paid closer attention when Hector kept going on about scriptures and entities.

"Have they told you nothing?" Anger flares in his eyes when he looks first at me, then over my shoulder at Eric.

"They may have." Shrugging again, I shuffle my feet self-consciously. "I was more interested in how to hit my mark than quoting passages and remembering names."

Rubbing his forehead as if I've given him a headache, Lucifer walks up to one of the sofas, plopping on it ungracefully. He was so composed until this very moment that it's startling to see him act almost normal. When he looks up at where I'm still standing like a human shield in front of Eric, he looks tired. Exhausted, actually.

"There were seven of us that fell first, as you would know it." Waving a hand, he prompts us to sit. Eric groans with his movement, pulling me with him and seating us both opposite Lucifer.

"The seven sins." He nods at me grimly.

"Beelzebub, Leviathan, Mammon, Asmodeous, Belphegor, Satanael, and me." One side of his lips lifts at the corner. "We didn't fall. Balance was needed if His creation was to continue. He chose us for this. Appointed each of us to rule our domains, me leading them all to keep order." At my skeptical look, he chuckles. "Chaos has the greatest order of them all."

My mind is spinning, trying to remember things that Hector spent days teaching me. "Your domain is pride."

"So it is." Nodding approvingly, that domain is unmistakable in his intent gaze. "Humans are simple creatures, and mistaking Satanael and me as one and the same made no difference."

"There is more to this. If you were chosen, why are you and the angels trying to kill each other?"

"I never said we didn't lose our way, forgetting why we are here. Forgetting who we are." Quicksilver shimmers through his eyes. "That is why Satanael and Sedakiel decided to create you. So you can help us remember and we find our way back to ourselves."

"Raphael said my father was a Demon of Wrath, and my mother an Angel of Mercy." My hand blindly reaches for Eric, and his fingers tangle with mine, anchoring me. Too many emotions are making me dizzy although I'm sitting down.

"Satanael's domain is Wrath." Tilting his head slightly, he zeroes in on the dagger still clutched in my hand. "Sedakiel, or you may have heard of her being called Zedkiel, is known as the Mercy of God." A genuine smile makes him look blindingly beautiful. He points his chin at my hand. "You carry the weapon she is well known for. Satanael has been keeping secrets, because I see his symbols on it, too."

Raking my brain, I frown at him. "Zedkiel is a man."

Laughter shakes his shoulders, pebbling my skin. "She

is all female, I assure you. She is no more a male than Satanael and I are one and the same. As I said, humans are simple creatures. Lost souls looking for redemption."

"Let's say I believe you." Everything in me believes every word he said, but I refuse to acknowledge it. "What's my purpose, apart from bleeding so you can waltz in through the gate on unsuspecting humans? To play a shepherd and guide you out of memory loss?" Snickering, I shift my butt uneasily on the sofa. "Here is Helena, therapist of the fallen. All appointments made right after you get your ass to Hell."

"Your blood can open any gate, you are made of both. Not just Hell." He looks insulted, and my brain screeches to a halt.

"What?" Lips parted, I gap at him. Eric's fingers tighten around mine, almost crushing my bones.

"Your blood can open the gate to Hell, or Heaven." Lucifer squares his shoulders, lifting slightly from his perch. "You look troubled."

"But Michael can go to Heaven whenever he wants," mumbling through numb lips, I can't even blink.

"Speak, girl."

Like a hawk, his focus is so intent I find myself spilling every thought and doubt that's been nagging me for weeks. "After Michael abducted me, I thought he would kill me so you can't use me to open the gate or keep it open. He didn't obviously, but I kept wondering the whole time I was locked up what was his point. I mean, how much blood does he need to keep Hell open long enough to face you in battle." Gulping air, I prepare myself to continue talking. Lucifer jumps angrily from the sofa, and I almost swallow my tongue.

"Mammon will cease to exist for this!" Spinning around, he roars, causing my ears to ring. "Colt!" The doors burst open, Colt shouldering his way through them, poised to fight. "Call Leviathan. I was right, the bastard is using jinn."

Eric jumps up, a painful grunt coming from him. Not knowing what is going on, I look at all of them, ignoring the Trowe that decides to yank on my hand at that moment.

"Jinn?" The dread in Eric's question curdles the blood in my veins.

"What the hell is a jinn?" Grabbing his hand, I jerk him towards me. "What's going on?"

"Jinn are shapeshifters." All the life drains from me before he is done talking. "If Mammon is using jinn, it may not have been Michael that held you prisoner for two weeks."

Chapter Fourteen

"That's bullshit, and you know it!" Jumping up as well, I whirl on Eric. "He was inside Sanctuary when I first met him. With all Elders present, might I remind you. The wards were strong enough to prevent that."

"The same wards that prevented me?" Distractingly, he glances at me, then turns to watch his brother bolt out of the room like his ass is on fire. "I was there, too."

Scrubbing a hand over my face angrily, I blow out a breath through puffed out cheeks like a chipmunk. Lucifer starts pacing in front of the roaring fireplace, adding to my anxiety. At least he forgot about wanting to kill Eric, or sever our bond. I might've been troubled by the fact I had no say in becoming his mate, but that doesn't mean I want anyone cutting it. With or without choice, it's mine. Plus, I almost said the L word earlier.

There is that.

"Let me get this straight." Wrapping my fingers around Eric's forearm, I turn him towards me until our gazes lock. "What you are telling me is, this started long before Michael showed up to tell me that I'm dead meat?" When his lips press into a thin, white line, my stomach jumps in my throat before dropping at my feet. "Is it one jinn? Please say it's only one of those bastards, or I'm going to die of tachycardia right now."

"It's not one." Lucifer chirps while continuing to wear a path in the floor, ignoring all of us.

"Nobody asked you." Snapping at him, I don't look away from Eric, begging him to contradict the jerk that is trying to kill me with words while not even looking my way.

"I should've suspected it." Eric gets on my shit list, agreeing with his father. I should've let Lucifer kill him. "It makes me wonder what Mammon has promised to get them involved in this."

"Now you are interested in comings and goings in my realm?" Like a dark cloud, Lucifer is pacing one second, and the next he is looming over Eric.

It's not a conscious decision when my dagger is pressed under his chin. Finding myself plastered to Lucifer's chest, I snarl at him. "I wanna know what's going on, who these jinn are and how I can send them back here and out of my world. Let's concentrate on that, huh? And unless you are planning on killing me first, get out of his face. Eric will not be dying by your hand. Not if I can help it."

"You have chosen well." Excitement sparkles in Lucifer's gaze, replacing the rage. "If I wanted to kill my own son, he would not be standing here, girl. He needed a lesson, one I thought he learned a long time ago." Slowly he pulls away from me, turning to look at the glass frame holding the mesmerizing wings above the mantel. "I had to be certain he is willing to protect you at all costs. That he will not turn his back when you need him like he has done to me."

"Oh, well"—Pitching my voice to sound like I'm a bubblehead with no brain, I continue pissing him off if the clenched fists at his sides are anything to go by—"that explains everything." Eric frowns, watching me warily, and Lucifer only turns his head my way. They both look like they've never seen me in their life. Good! "You see, you are a jerk that likes to push people around. I wouldn't stick around either. Me, on the other hand, I have a vagina. It trumps being an ass any day."

Lucifer opens his mouth, then closes it with a snap, turning his attention to Eric with his brow up in an arch. "Did she get damaged when you passed through the portal? She seemed lucid to this point."

Lips twitching, Eric's green eyes soften and twinkle

when he looks at me. I want to slap him. "My mate has a temper." Lucifer grunts as if that explains everything.

"First of all,"—Pointing the blade at Lucifer, I scowl at him—"that was not a nice thing to say. Second,"—The sharp, pointy thing turns Eric's way, making his grin broaden, the asshole.—"I have a temper only when I'm dealing with jerks who think little girl Helena needs to be told what to do, or when they are trying to kill me."

"Satanael will be proud." Lucifer keeps poking that little tidbit that I'm doing everything I can to ignore.

"And let's not talk about my parents." Crossing my arms over my chest, I purse my lips. Mature, I know. "Jinn. One of you was going to tell me about these jinn bastards." The Trowe chuckles gleefully. A creepy sound that almost makes me jump out of my skin. I forgot about him.

"Go fetch Beelzebub." Power blasts the Trowe when Lucifer addresses him, singeing my skin.

The creature whimpers, baring his teeth. "I don't serve you, Lucifer." Hissing, he crawls on all fours, stopping at my feet. "I have a mistress now."

Eric laughs, covering it with a cough at Lucifer's thunderous scowl.

The fact that the creature disobeyed Lucifer makes me giddy. I'm disturbed by its presence and attachment to me, nonetheless. "Yes, Lucifer. He has a mistress now." Baring my own teeth in a mockery of a smile, I nudge the Trowe with my foot. "Go, do what he asked."

With a squeal, the creature disappears from the room, the banging of the door slamming shut is the only thing proving he was even in the place. I didn't know it could move like that. Then again, I don't know anything about him or anything else here by the looks of it. That brings my thoughts back to what we were discussing before I got sidetracked, as usual.

"Now that no one is trying to kill each other, and apparently we are waiting; can anyone explain to me what exactly is going on." I start moving back to my sofa but think better of it. Snatching Eric's arm, I drag him with me, away from Lucifer. Plopping us both on the soft cushions, I raise my eyebrows at the fallen angel watching us with amusement. "You were telling me about the jinn. What kind of demons are we talking about here?"

"Not demons." Following our example, Lucifer gingerly sits opposite us. I'm happy his chair got smashed to splinters because it makes me feel more on equal ground like this. "Not exactly. They are separate from both realms. Created to keep us on track with our tasks. The Creator uses them as spies. They are his eyes and ears in all the realms." Both his brows dip, forming a V between his eyes. "They never should've gotten involved in this mess."

"I can't see what Mammon can promise to make them agree to get involved." Eric muses next to me, staring unseeing at the flames of the fireplace.

"What's Mammon's domain?" Feeling lost, I glance at Eric. Lucifer answers me.

"Greed."

"How appropriate." Drawling dryly, my mouth twists in a grimace. "I should've guessed." Spearing my fingers through my hair, I grab a fistful, yanking on it to clear the hundreds of thoughts floating in my head. "I'd think some of us would've noticed if we are faced with anything other than what we can see, no?" Alternating between Lucifer and Eric, I search their faces for clues. "I mean, Michael used his powers. Surely these jinn have a tell we can use to identify them. Right?"

"Not necessarily." Lucifer sighs, his words spoken cautiously. "One must be aware such a thing is in the works so we can look for tells. They were created to mimic any of us perfectly."

"What you are telling me is that anyone can be a jinn and not who we think they are?" Stupid hope unfurls in my chest. "Maybe Amanda and Hector were jinn? Jared?" I'm too afraid to turn to Eric, so he doesn't destroy the fragile idea blooming inside me.

"Not Hector, no." Regardless that I ignore him, he still opens his mouth. "He smelled too much like a human to be anything but." Tilting his head left and right, not seeing my glare, he scratches the stubble on his jaw. "I can't be sure about your friend. I didn't pay her that much attention considering the situation."

"Judging by this conversation, anyone can be a jinn."

As soon as the words pass my lips, I jump away from Eric, stabbing the air in his direction with my dagger. "You could be a jinn, too." He jerks back like the blade pierced his skin. "You've been acting weird ever since we got here."

"He is not a jinn, I assure you." Arrogance oozes out of Lucifer when he looks at me with annoyance. "He is acting strange because of meeting with me after so long I would assume." Giving Eric a flick of his eyes, he leans back on the sofa he is occupying. "We didn't leave things on good terms last time we were in the same room." Pointedly, he looks at the glass case with the wings.

A chasm opens in my gut.

"Whose wings are those?" Dread makes my question sound timid.

If I weren't watching Lucifer so intently, I would've missed the guilt flashing fast in his eyes, and the slight downward curl of his lips. The tension in the air around us reaches whole new levels, making it a chore to drag a lungful of oxygen in.

"Mine."

For the first time since we dropped in this hole of a place, I feel Eric's emotions like they are my own. Pain, not physical, more profound than even emotional scarring, stabs me in the center of my chest, leaving me breathless.

Chapter Fifteen

"Bullshit." Blurting the first thing that comes to mind, the anger spikes up inside me. "No, they are not."

Eric stiffens, closing my mouth faster than if he placed his hand on it. Swallowing everything else I wanted to say, I make sure he sees that he has a shit ton of explaining to do. Lucifer watches us both through narrowed eyes like he can read the unspoken conversation. Pedaling back to remove the foot from my mouth, I look away from monster boy.

"I'm sure he would've told me if he had wings." *Act stupid Hel,* I tell myself while blinking at Lucifer.

"I have made mistakes in my anger." Murmuring, Lucifer turns his full focus on Eric. "You always did have a talent for bringing the worst out in me."

"Says every psycho to those they hurt." The ground under my feet trembles violently in beat with my anger.

Lucifer opens his mouth, turning to me with fury burning in his gaze. The door bangs loudly open a moment before small hands latch around my leg. Acting on impulse, I grab a handful of hair, snatching whatever it is that attached itself to me and swinging my right leg, kicking it like a ball aiming at the fireplace. Something small flies right in the center of the fire.

Whatever it was that Lucifer was about to say turns into a deep belly laugh. A shriek makes my ears bleed, and I stumble back, covering them. The Trowe jumps out of the fire rolling around, shrieking while doing his best not to burn alive. Panic compresses my chest, and I slide the dagger to the small of my back. Grabbing the first thing I can think of, the pretty rug in front of the fireplace, I start pelting him with it. The harsh scent of burning hair and roasted skin rolls my stomach, but I keep hitting him with the rug until the flames are no longer covering him. The burning stops but the laughter continues. Even Eric is laughing, the asshole.

"Not funny!" My snapping only makes them laugh harder, so I turn to the Trowe. "What were you thinking? I told you touching me like that can get you killed!"

"Sorry mistress." The creature rasps miserably, blisters, and charred skin smoking around him. My gut clenches at the sight.

"Eric, when you have a moment to stop laughing, will you help him?" Glaring, I point a finger at the creature. "Like now, for example."

"He'll be fine." Chuckling, he bites on his lips, but his shoulders keep shaking, pissing me off.

"He is not fine!" Doing my best not to look at the Trowe, I slam my fists on my hips. "I see you've healed nicely. I almost killed my sidekick. Do something."

"Sidekick?" Lucifer asks, arching an eyebrow and finally not laughing his ass off.

"Yeah, well, I don't see any of you jumping to do everything I ask, now do I? Will you help him?"

I don't ask if he can. I know he can.

With his calculating gaze locked on me, Lucifer twirls his fingers, sending tendrils of darkness at the Trowe. I keep watching his face, not willing to see what he is doing. As long as he fixes the result of my kneejerk reaction, I'm good with whatever it is. The relief I hear when the Trowe sighs forces me to turn to the creature. He is sprawled like a starfish in all his ugly glory on the floor. No sight of burned skin or hair is visible, releasing the pressure in my chest.

"Thank you." I keep staring at the creature, uncomfortable with thanking Lucifer.

"I must admit, if I knew how entertaining my day would become, I would've come sooner." The booming voice coming from the doorway has me clutching the dagger in my hand again.

The newcomer leaning his shoulder on the doorframe can only be described as a mountain of a man. Where Lucifer looks like a lean, mean, killing machine, this guy can definitely pick things up, put them down, all while picking his white sparkling teeth with one of the ancient tree trunks we used for cover before we got here. Where the ruler of Hell oozes sophistication and elegance, brute force watches me from the doorway with curiosity.

Easily at seven feet, muscled arms with biceps as wide as my waist are crossed over his broad chest. The fabric of the black t-shirt is stretched within an inch of its life on his torso. Black Sabbath is written in blood-red letters with a silhouette of a demoness sitting at the center of his pecks. Multipocketed tactical gear pants wrap around muscled legs, ending with shitkickers on his large feet. Tattoos cover his bare arms and peek from the collar of his t-shirt towards his neck. His military hair cut makes his pretty features harsher, moving him from handsome to hot as fuck. Only the red eyes glittering with amusement at my perusal can warn an unsuspecting person of the danger that surrounds this guy like a second skin.

My mouth dries up like the Sahara Desert.

"Beelzebub," the damn Trowe says excitedly, making me flinch. I almost kick him back in the fire for forcing me to react and show weakness in front of everyone here. Stupid creature.

"Narsi." Beelzebub grins at my sidekick. "I didn't expect to see you here."

"It has a name?" Gaping at the Trowe, I blink fast. "You have a name?"

"Of course, it has a name," Lucifer says patronizingly making me bristle.

"Excuse the fuck out of me for not stopping to ask while I'm running away from Archangels trying to kill me and dropping in Hell like it's the newest hot spot for tourists."

Lucifer frowns disapprovingly at me while Eric and Beelzebub turn red in the face, their shoulders twitching from suppressed laughter. The anger that has been bubbling inside me and keeps pushing to the surface takes that opportunity to hit a new high, shaking the entire monstrosity of a building like it's been hit by a rocket launcher. Eric is off the sofa, wrapping his arms around me before I can register what just happened.

"Hel, I'm here. Just breathe." Pressing my face to his chest, he holds me tight.

The scent of his skin fills my nostrils, clearing my head. Circling his trim waist, I hold onto him to ground myself and pull away from the blinding emotion that made me see everything bathed in red. Beelzebub whistles low.

"What is happening to me, Eric?" Pressing closer to him, I do my best to hide how freaked out I am.

My entire body is trembling, muscles twitching under Eric's arms. If he notices, he doesn't say a word. He just holds me in the circle of his arms, lending me strength. It's moments like this that allow me to forgive him everything when he is a jerk.

"Her blood is adjusting to the powers she inherited from Satanael." Lucifer takes on the condescending tone I heard a few times already. "It'll pass." He dismisses my torment, nonchalantly.

"I should've known it's Satanael's daughter." Beelzebub finally peels himself off the doorframe and saunters in the room.

"We have other pressing matters." Turning away from us, Lucifer looks at Beelzebub. "Mammon is using jinn."

"What?" Stumbling, Beelzebub gawks at all of us in turn. "How? Where did you hear this? That's impossible!"

"It's why I summoned you." Lifting up, Lucifer faces the other fallen. "We need to speak to Abaddon. If I go myself, I will destroy him before I hear what he has to say for himself. His name is mentioned more than I like in this mess."

"I thought Lilith was in charge of him." Everyone turns to me. "What? Maddison said he was given to her by her mother." Shrugging a shoulder, I turn to look at the Trowe, so I don't squirm under their penetrating gazes.

"I will not involve Lilith unless I must. She has too much pent-up aggression when it comes to Mammon. Before we set him in her sights, we need to figure out what he has been plotting." Lucifer and Beelzebub grin knowingly at each other like high school boys.

"Weirdos!" Mumbling, I raise both eyebrows at Eric.

His lips curl up slightly, and he winks at me. Butterflies unfurl in my belly when I become aware of his skin surrounding me. His nostrils flare and hunger burns in his gaze, the amber eating up the green color of his eyes. I'm mortified when Lucifer and Beelzebub inhale loudly as well. With my face turning all shades of red, I clear my throat.

"What are we waiting for? Let's go find Abaddon. I really don't want to be here longer than I must."

"We are waiting for Leviathan." A knowing smile graces Lucifer's lips, and I wish the ground would split open again to swallow me whole.

"Your messenger boy sucks, dude."

I should've known that as soon as I say that Colt will show up at the door. Baring my teeth at him in the resemblance of a smile only makes him glare more. Eric snorts, smirking at his brother, so I stomp on his foot. A displeased growl rumbles his chest while Lucifer shakes his head at us like we are misbehaving children.

"He said to meet him at the gates." Turning away from us, Colt addresses his father. "We have incoming in less than thirty minutes." We all straighten up at that. "A horde is headed our way." Flicking his gaze at me, his lips thin out. "They know the girl is here."

"Damn it!" Groaning, I thump my forehead off Eric's chest.

Chapter Sixteen

Eric

Thinking I can get Helena out of here before something like this happens is too optimistic on my part. I like it when I'm a step ahead of a situation, but ever since the she-devil stormed into my life, I've been acting on impulse instead of calculated decisions. Her life is spiraling out of control, and I'm hurled along with it. The consequences could be dire for both of us if I don't get my shit together.

"How bad is it?" Helena looks at me when my father, Colt, and Beelzebub storm out of the room.

"He has an army stashed in this place at his disposal."

Grabbing her face between my palms, I take advantage of the moment we have alone to press my lips to hers. "No one will hurt you, Hel."

"While we have a chance"—Pulling away from me, she glances at the fireplace—"wanna explain how your wings ended up in two places at once?"

Inhaling deeply, I look at them as well. "I don't have an answer, Hel. On this one, I'm just as lost as you." Subconsciously, I roll my shoulders, testing the feeling in case I imagined it. The weighted pressure indicating my folded hidden wings assures me it wasn't a dream. "I never thought I'd feel them again after my father removed them."

"You don't want him to know that you have them back." It's not a question.

"I don't want him knowing what led to me having them back. There is a difference." Grabbing her by the shoulders, I force her to look at me. "No matter how accommodating or helpful they all are. My father, Raphael, whoever it may be. They all have their own agendas, and I'll be damned if I let them use you as a pawn for their schemes."

"Thank you." Lifting on her tiptoes, she pecks my lips, "I can't say I'm happy to be here, but at least he is more forthcoming with information. The Holy assess are tightlipped. We know a lot more so we can be ready for whatever comes."

"If he is willing to share, he expects to gain something

from it." Taking her hand, I lead us out of the room. "We better get moving so we can hear everything they say."

"Paranoid much?" Snickering, she follows without question. My chest feels tight at the trust she is giving me. "I thought that was my job to be suspicious of everyone."

"When it comes to you, I'm suspicious even of myself." Twisting us through the hallways, I watch her from the corner of my eye. "I'm not taking chances."

Nodding, Helena doesn't lift her head as she scans the little fires illuminating the floors. The scattering of feet announces the Haltija we left sprawled on the floor catching up to us. After almost burning to death, he makes sure she can hear him move now. Biting the inside of my mouth so I don't smile, I watch him shuffle around us like a dog on all fours.

Oppressing thoughts try to push me to my knees, memories of this place that I've buried so deep I thought they'd never find their way to torment me again. The air starts burning my lungs, the stench of sweat and blood so vivid I glance at my arms to make sure I'm not bleeding. My father's voice booms in my ears, "Get up you pathetic shit. You are my blood, you never kneel."

Claws push from my fingertips, alerting Helena of my mental state. Grinding my teeth, I force them back, not daring to look at her. If I see disgust or fear in her expressive eyes, it'll gut me. Or even worse, pity. Lengthening my stride, I almost run out of the front door. After the warm fresh air blasts my face, I become aware that Helena didn't say a word.

She didn't demand to know what's going on, nor did she stop asking what's up my ass. She is still clutching my hand, her tiny fingers digging in my skin. I don't deserve her understanding, compassion, or loyalty. I want it and will hold onto it till my last breath, but I don't deserve it.

I don't deserve her.

"How good of you to join us," Colt snarls at me.

"How about you mind your damn business dumbass, before I knock your ass over again, huh?" I've never heard Helena growl like a beast before. Even my father and Beelzebub turn to her in shock.

"You have women fighting your battles now?" Colt snarls at me but takes a step back from her with his arms lifted at his sides.

"Are we sure he is not a jinn?" Helena glances at me. "I can stick the pointy bit of my dagger right between his eyes just to make sure."

"Colt is suffering from personal inadequacy, I'm afraid." Pulling her back, I give him a glare. "We have other problems to deal with. He can handle his own."

"We should keep the girl inside." As soon as Beelzebub turns to my father, I tighten my hold on Helena.

"The girl is right here, you ass, and you can talk to her directly." Yanking her arm, she does her best to dislodge me. Launching herself at Beelzebub, I manage to snatch her by the waist before she gets too far. "No one is keeping me anywhere."

"All of you act like you've never dealt with a female in your existence." Frustrated that they keep on angering her, she almost slips away.

"And you became an expert when exactly?" Beelzebub turns to me incredulously.

"When I shot him in the ass." Helena grins proudly. "Well, in his upper thigh, but it was close."

With a groan, I keep her from stabbing anyone while the three of them laugh. Even the damn Haltija is chuckling, sounding deranged. I almost crush her arms when her body goes slack, and she stops struggling. Expecting Mammon's lackeys to already be within sight, I turn to face them, pushing her behind me.

"Holy shit!" Helena blurts, and grabbing my hand, she drags me towards the front doors. "That's a jinn?" Her eyes are too large on her face, and she puts more speed into her movements. "Get inside, all of you. That thing messes with your head."

Confused at her panic, I let her pull me along, turning to look over my shoulder. When I see what has her concerned, I wish this day will end so I can have a fresh start to make things right. The smirk on my father's face makes me want to punch him.

"Hel, stop." Pulling her back, I prevent her from going further. "It's not a jinn."

"It's that dragon thing, Eric." Snapping, she tries to

hide the hurt, but I see it clearly. “I have no desire to feel like my skin is melting off my bones.” Flinching, she scrunches up her button nose at the Trowe. “Sorry.”

“What is she talking about?” Of course my father will want to get involved with this.

“Yes, Eric. Do tell. What is she talking about?” Colt, not wanting to miss an opportunity to piss me off, looks triumphant.

“I had no intention of coming here.” Pushing the words through clenched teeth, I don’t dare to look at Helena. “If I had it my way, we would’ve been back in the human realm while the rest of you stayed oblivious of our presence here. I didn't think when we passed through the portal that we’d end up so close to the palace. It must’ve triggered the wards because we were almost spotted a few minutes after stepping foot through the gate.”

“I see.” My father’s face slips into the mask of indifference he shows to everyone. I’ve known him long enough to be able to see the disappointment and anger burning bright in his gaze. “You used the girl to hide your presence.” One sharp nod is all I can give.

The ground rocks when the black dragon drops in the courtyard. Obsidian scales glimmer in the moonlight, the long neck swiveling side to side until the head tilts sideways and a vertical yellow pupil shrinks and expands, taking us in. Helena steps next to me, taking my hand in her sweat-sleeked palm. Guilt eats a hole in my gut for adding to her anxiety.

"If it starts messing with my head, I'm going to charge and stab the shit out of it." Murmuring under her breath, she doesn't look my way.

The dragon chuckles.

A sound, like rolling rocks down a hillside, vibrates the ground and I feel it through my feet. When the head lowers at eye level, Helena stiffens. Blowing out a breath, I rub my face with my hand roughly.

"Hel, this is Leviathan."

Her head very slowly turns my way, and I take a full step away from her. It was a big mistake placing me in a perfect range. Her eyes narrow to slits, and before I realize what she is doing, she executes an ideal round kick, slamming her boot in my jaw. My head snaps back, my body following the strength of the hit, sending me flying into the wall. When I hit the ground on my hands and knees, I hear Lucifer, Leviathan, and Beelzebub laugh. I'm surprised Colt hasn't joined them.

The bastards.

Chapter Seventeen

Helena

I'm so angry at Eric at this moment that I'm finding it hard not to just stab him in the chest and keep going until I have no energy left to lift my arm. Not because he hid from someone that apparently had no intention of harming him, but only because it gets on my nerves that he is tightlipped about everything.

I can tell he is dealing with something internal, this damn place making him act almost depressed and brooding, and I get that. God knows I haven't talked about all my triggers and issues with him, either. What gets me so angry with him is the longer he stays quiet the more it feels like he doesn't trust me. Or sees me as an outsider in this unusual duo we created. While I look at things as us against them, his behavior says him against everything, including me.

This needs to stop. Like, now.

"I deserved that." Lifting up, he dusts off his knees.

"No shit you deserved it." Clutching the dagger, I glare at him. "I'm trying very hard not to stab you right now."

Watching him fidget and look anywhere else but at me, I don't notice the dragon moving until a puff of hot, stinking breath ruffles my hair. Jumping away from it, my hand slashes the air by reflex, and the dagger slides through rough scales like they were butter, leaving scratches on my knuckles. I get tackled to the side, my hip and shoulder hitting the unforgiving ground. Sharp pain shoots through my body rattling my teeth, just as a blast of fire bursts in the spot I was occupying a second ago. An earsplitting roar follows the flames leaving me deaf to anything else but the blood pounding in my ears.

"Holy shit!" I can't hear myself, but Eric flinches, which tells me I must've shouted the words right in his ear. His limbs are tangled with mine on the ground.

Shoving my shoulder in his chest, I roll us around so that I'm on top of him. His fingers are wrapped around my wrist, keeping my hand still holding the dagger away. I can't hear a thing, so I sit straddling Eric's chest, watching Lucifer and Beelzebub talk animatedly to the dragon. Leviathan's head is swiveling angrily, black blood dripping from his snout to the reddish dust at his feet. That's one nasty gash I made at the center of his nose, splitting the scales right between the two large nostrils that keep flaring from his fury.

My heart is still jackhammering in my chest, slowing down slowly with each stroke of Eric's hands on my thighs. Panting, I look down at him, no doubt my eyes wide enough to look like they're about to pop out of their sockets. I watch his lips move to form the word breathe, so I follow the advice. Sounds trickle to my ears, getting louder with each word spoken.

"Shift." The distorted voice of Lucifer turns my head his way.

Red light bursts around the dragon, searing my retinas. Blinking hurts while hot tears run unchecked down my cheeks, splattering over Eric's chest. When I'm finally able to squint without wanting to cry out in pain, I see a man crouched on the ground where the dragon used to be.

I'm struck dumb for few seconds when a head full of thick blond hair lifts up and another too perfect to be human face turns my way. Glacial blue eyes pierce my gaze, the intensity of the look enough to make me jerk back like it's a physical blow. There is no sight from the open gash the dragon had. High cheekbones stretch his alabaster skin, a little crooked nose that must've been broken too many times to stay like that on a fallen angel, sitting above firmly pressed lips. His square jaw is covered in stubble, adding to the wild look his mussed hair is giving off. Bare-chested in only leather pants, he is crouched like a feline ready to pounce and devour the mouse. Me being the mouse in this case. Muscles ripple under his skin like someone is holding him back from attacking me. There is nothing human in this person. At least all the angels I've met so far, fallen or not, mimicked human expressions or speech. Not Leviathan. He is all wild beast.

Untamed.

"You can stop staring at my mate," Eric speaks, and I'm happy that my hearing is back to normal even when my eyes still feel dry, and my eyelids are like sandpaper every time I blink. "You asked for it, there was no need to get in her face like that while she was distracted."

"What he said." Pushing off Eric, I get on my feet, pulling him along with me. "Everyone needs to stay out of my personal bubble. We saw what happens when I get startled." Not mentioning that I need to stop being so jumpy, I frown at the still crouching fallen. "What's wrong with him?"

"I will hold him frozen until he calms down," Lucifer snaps at his buddy.

"We are getting off track here. I can feel them getting closer." Beelzebub turns his back on all of us and walks up to the closed iron gates. Stopping a couple of feet in front of them, he looks over his shoulder. How he manages to do that with a neck as thick as my thigh, I have no idea. “Can we do this first? We can try to kill each other later.”

Grateful for the break in tension around us, I hurry to join him. “I’m with him.” I can feel Eric following close behind me, the heat of his body warming my back. “What are we doing exactly?” When I stop next to Beelzebub, I mumble the question so the other two jerks don’t hear. I’m hoping he will say we face whoever is coming because I’m brimming with pent-up aggression, itching for a fight.

“You do nothing.” His lips twitch at the corners when he looks down at me. “The three of us will place wards. No one will cross these gates unless we want them here.”

“No one?” Craning my neck to keep eye contact, I show my skepticism. “Not even Mammon?”

“Not even Mammon can breach wards placed by the three of us together.” I grin at him, and he chuckles. “I like her.” Beelzebub looks over my head at Eric.

“She has that effect on people.” The humor is evident in Eric’s voice.

“That does not sound as comforting as you may think.” Murmuring under my breath, I do my best not to smile when Beelzebub throws his head back and laughs.

Ignoring the amused look Lucifer is throwing my way, I square my shoulders and walk like I own the place.

Now that is a disturbing thought.

Chapter Eighteen

Backing away, Eric and I join Colt, who has been brooding mutely near the front doors of Lucifer's home the entire time. I can feel him tracking my movements, but ignoring him is better than arguing pointlessly. It's obvious he and Eric have some old wounds they need to deal with. I have no intention of getting in the middle of that. Staying alive and dealing with my own problems takes priority.

Leviathan and Lucifer must've come to an agreement. Both of them join Beelzebub at the gates, albeit walking stiffly, like the sticks up their asses are rubbing them wrong. I watch fascinated as they spread away from each other, each of them facing away from the other two. When their hands lift to the sides like they are trying to embrace the realm by thought alone, thickness saturates the atmosphere around us. The air flowing through my nostrils is trickling sluggishly like molasses. Parting my lips, I drag in gulps of oxygen, not daring to blink in case I miss something. Beelzebub's words echo in my head. "No one will cross these gates unless we want them here." Uneasiness crawls like spiders up my spine. How about leaving? Can I leave this place after they have the wards up?

Always anticipating my mental state, Eric twines his fingers with mine. The reassuring squeeze he gives me doesn't help put away my troubling thoughts, but it's something at least. Returning the gesture, I keep watching the three fallen work. Power blasts from all of them, circling around the area like a sentient being. Expecting it to close around us like a dome, I'm startled when I feel the prodding of invisible fingers in my head and chest. Even my butt cheeks clench at the intrusive feeling, alarms blaring inside me telling me to get the hell out of there.

"It's the wards, Hel. I promise I won't let anyone hurt you. If you believe nothing else from me after everything I've done, believe that." Eric calms my fight or flight instinct enough to keep me rooted to the spot.

"It's not that I don't believe you, Eric." Giving him a side-eye, I keep facing forward. "All this is getting to be a bit too much to deal with all at once. And you doing everything you said you won't do is not helping at all."

"I know." I can feel the tension in his body. "Saying I'm sorry won't cut it. I should give you more credit and let you decide. Even if it means you'll never look at me the same. Even if it means I'll have a mate that wants nothing to do with me. It will kill me, but I promise I will give you that choice." Shaking his head, he chuckles bitterly. "Everything I thought I buried and left behind is coming to bite me in the ass so fast my head is spinning."

"Look." Holding back my words, I point beyond the iron gates.

A cloud of darkness shows on the horizon, closing in fast. No, not a cloud. My brain numbs when I see the sea of demons approaching us at speed. Their numbers blot out the bright silvery light of the pregnant moon hanging so low in the starless sky I can reach out and touch it. A feeling of dread overrides every other emotion I have, pushing Eric's words to the back of my mind for a later date.

They won't have enough time to stop them.

Looking at the three fallen, I can clearly see their arms trembling slightly, tightening my gut. The power keeps swirling, seeming more interested in me than saving our asses from whatever is coming for our heads. Colt bolts out of his spot to join the others, similar shadows like I've seen Eric have flowing from his hands. When Eric hesitates, I release his hand, urging him to do something.

Anything really, as long as we survive this night. He joins the rest, leaving me quaking in my boots.

"Come on, come on…" repeating it like a mantra, the dagger almost slips from my sweaty palm.

Guilt eats a hole in my stomach that I'm standing here feeling useless while leaving others to keep me safe. It's not something I'm used to feeling. It's always been me facing whatever danger lurks in the shadows so I can protect everyone else. Even recklessly, some may say. But here I am. Standing in Lucifer's front yard, waiting on him and two other fallen angels to keep me alive. The Heaven's hunter relying on Hell's help to keep breathing. The irony of it tastes bitter on my tongue. This is all wrong. It should've been Archangels protecting me instead of wanting me dead. How did I find myself in this alternate universe where nothing makes sense anymore? I can't dwell on that for long thankfully.

We are running out of time.

I can distinguish the twisted, snarling faces of the demons charging us, foam gathering at the corners of their mouths and dripping down their chins. They are so close now that we'll be face to face within minutes. The quiet that surrounds us gets broken by the singing sound of metal leaving a sheath. Goosebumps cover my whole body, adrenaline pumping through my veins in sync with the galloping of my heart. The ground shaking violently makes me stumble, blinking away the sweat running in rivulets down my face.

They are too close.

A broad sword glints, reflecting the light of the moon on its blade, pulling my attention to it. The demon gripping the weapon grins menacingly, swinging his arm back, releasing it in the air. Everything around me moves in slow motion, the whooshing sound of the flipping blade in the air becoming part of me. I can almost feel the wind through which it flies like it's touching my skin. Following its path, I finally see the target that it's aiming for. The target that it's going to hit right in the center of the chest.

Eric.

"NO!"

The scream that is ripped from the bottom of my soul spreads around us with so much intensity it sends everyone, including the men trying to keep us alive, on their knees. The demons running at full speed trip and tumble all over each other, creating mountains of tangled limbs as roars of anger and pain join my voice. Heat that I'm sure will burn me alive blasts from my body like a nuclear bomb going off, bathing everything I see in hues of gold and red. I feel the consciousness leaving me, and I fight it with everything I am.

If I'm going to die here in the pits of Hell, I will die standing, looking my murderer in the eye. No matter what I do and how much I want that to be true, darkness crawls at the corners of my eyes. My vision tunnels and the silvery light of the moon gets smaller and smaller until just a pinprick of it is left, taunting me.

And then I feel it.

Like a snapping rubber band, the power that was aimlessly swirling around us snaps closed. The twirling sword in the air hits it at full speed, disintegrating to ash on contact, leaving deathly silence in its wake. It takes the pinprick of light with it, and I collapse on the ground.

Chapter Nineteen

Eric

"I can try to heal her." For the fiftieth time, my father offers the same thing.

"No, she won't like that, and unless she specifically agrees on anything, I'm not making decisions for her again."

She's been sleeping for two days now. The pads of my fingers stay pressed on her wrist, feeling the pulse of her vein the entire time. I can hear her heartbeat as loud as my own, but it makes me feel calmer when I'm touching her.

When she sealed the wards like nothing I've ever seen before, she collapsed on the ground, pale and lifeless like a corpse and I almost turned feral. Colt reached her first, standing closer to where she was before I was able to get to her. I'm not sure what exactly happened, remembering only bits and pieces of his body going limp and my claws being wrapped around his throat. The rest of them stayed away, lingering at a safe distance while my father watched me warily. The fact that my wings were unfurled, stretched out like a shield around Helena with me crouching and snarling next to her might have something to do with it.

I haven't seen my brother after Beelzebub carried him away, nor have I asked about him. He should know better than to touch my mate. If he didn't, I'm sure he does now. We have always snapped at each other's ankles like rabid dogs, but this is different. Whatever he's been festering on, it's between him and me, and he should leave Helena out of it.

"If nothing else, I might bring her around. She should've been up by now." My father keeps pushing, unaware of my dark thoughts. Or because of them. I wouldn't put it past him.

"She will come around when she is ready." Squeezing the words through clenched teeth, I flare my nostrils, sucking a breath in to calm the rage down. "She expended too much power, and it needs time to replenish itself."

"She did it because she thought your life was in danger." Moving away from the threshold where he was leaning a shoulder on the doorframe, he comes closer to the bed where Helena has been unmoving for too long.

Saying nothing, I keep my focus on the rise and fall of her chest. My entire existence is centered on that movement. Heaven and Hell be damned. Shadows sneak up from my hands, caressing my mate's skin, willing her to open her eyes. It does no good, but I keep trying. I like to believe she wouldn't mind me sharing my energy with her.

"Colt recovered." Pushing his hands in the pockets of his pressed pants, my father is not deterred by my animosity towards him. "In case you were wondering."

"I wasn't."

The silence stretches between us. My skin itches, the rage spreading like an entity inside me as it looks for an outlet. The longer Helena stays sleeping, the more the fear fuels it, leading me to a breaking point. Not even Michael having her hidden pushed me this close to the edge.

"Your wings are back." And here it is. The reason he keeps circling me like a vulture for two days. It must chip at his pride that his punishment was thwarted.

"You can have them back"—Finally meeting his gaze, I can't stop the tired sigh—"if you just let me see to my mate in peace."

Eyebrows pulled low over his eyes, he watches me silently for a moment, as if taken aback by my comment. "I hold no hatred for you, Eric, nor was my punishment meant as such. I meant what I said to the girl, I have made mistakes when it comes to you."

"Can we not have this conversation now?" My temples develop a heartbeat of their own. "I was perfectly content without the wings. I'm willing to part with them again, as soon as I can take my mate out of here. It'll give you another decoration for the walls that surround you, to fill in the emptiness of this tomb you call home."

"I don't regret many things, as is my nature." Pressing the bridge of his nose, he stands like that long enough that I want to roar from the top of my lungs and tell him to get out of the room. "The way I handled things with you might be the only regret I have. Still"—Turning to me, his eyes flash with quicksilver—"I need to know how you got them back."

"I don't know." Forcing myself not to stiffen, my voice sounds bored.

"I know it has something to do with the girl; it's the only explanation." His focus stays on me like a hawk. "The how's and whys are something that can mean a turning point in all this mess Mammon got us in. Before it's too late." The last part is murmured, so I'm not even sure he meant to say it out loud.

"I said, I don't know." The words are barely audible pushed through a clenched jaw. "They showed up before I knew she existed."

"You lie!" Malice is apparent when he hisses at me.

"Prove it!" answering in kind, I grin at him like a fiend.

"I can do that easily." Glancing pointedly at Helena, he straightens up. "I have all the time now that we are all stuck here together."

"If you do anything to her"—Releasing my mate's hand, I lift to my full height, facing him—"you will see how well you have taught me to be exactly like you. Neither you nor I will survive that little tumble."

"I'm not your enemy, Eric." Shaking his head, he walks away, stopping at the threshold where this whole conversation started. "You fear for her, and I should let you calm down before you can see reason. The girl has nothing to fear from me; neither do you." Throwing those words with his back turned to me, he walks out, closing the door behind him.

Breathing harshly, air whizzing through my nostrils like a raging bull, I clench my fists into a white-knuckled grip. I don't trust him, or the angels around Helena, and nothing any of them say will change that. Even if she decides to turn her back on me after everything, I will follow her. I'll be her shadow for as long as I breathe to make sure she is safe from all of them.

"I screwed up again, didn't I?" Helena's whisper is raspy and raw. She coughs weakly when I kneel at her bedside.

"You are awake." With shaking hands, I smooth the hair around her face. "You did nothing wrong."

"I'll start thinking I scared you, monster boy." Lips lifting in a sleepy smile, she squints at me. "I'm guessing the wards held them back?"

"You saved the day, cupcake." Pressing my lips to hers, I inhale her scent. "They'll know better than to mess with you now."

"I'm going to tell Lucifer that because of me your wings are back."

"You'll do no such thing." Holding her face between my palms, I force her to look at me. "What you do, what you can do, none of them need to know. In these fucked up worlds, you need to keep your powers close to your skin. I'll be dead before I allow them to use you."

"Okay." Her eyelids flutter closed, leaving me to wonder if she was aware of what she was saying.

"At least she woke up," I tell myself, pressing my forehead to hers.

Chapter Twenty

Helena

"You would think they'd eventually give up." Pointing my chin at the demons throwing themselves bodily at the wards and sending sparks everywhere, I glance at Eric.

It took an additional twenty-four hours after I spoke to him to fully wake up. With the time spent learning stuff from Lucifer, stabbing dragons and almost burning my sidekick to a crisp before going nuclear on their asses, I've spent four days in Hell. That's three days, twenty-three hours, and fifty-five minutes more than I wanted to be here. Without a word, Eric stops next to me at the front doors, yanking me roughly to his side.

Not Eric then.

"Colt, I think I told you I'd stab you in the forehead if you kept doing this." Shoving him away, I glare at him. "No one thinks it's funny."

"I find it interesting that you can't tell which one of us is your mate unless we speak." Smirking, he leers, pissing me off.

"If you can't see how pathetic this makes you look, maybe they've dropped you on your head when you were born." Scrunching up my face, I pretend like I'm looking for a bump still on his head. "Is that why you feel inferior to Eric?"

My back hits the wall, Colt getting in my face, sneering "Careful little girl, anything can happen when no one is watching." A shiver of revulsion passes through me when he grinds his erection on my lower belly, pinning my arms between us.

Pushing the bile rising in my throat down, I grin at him. I was expecting him to do something like this by now. "You have no idea how right you are about that, asshole." His eyes bulge out, and he freezes when I press the dagger harder at his groin. "You think there is anything here worth chopping off?" Acting like I'm thinking on it, I move my head left and right slightly. "I think not, but I'm willing to give it a go."

"What is the meaning of this?" Beelzebub booms from

somewhere behind Colt, his deep voice echoing in the empty hallway.

"Just Colt making sure I don't fall down." With a fiendish smile, I wink at Colt. "I felt a little dizzy."

Backing away slowly, Eric's brother whirls around and storms outside through the still open doors. Too bad for the wards, I wouldn't mind those feral demons snacking on him right now.

"You alright, Helena?" Coming closer but still keeping his distance, Beelzebub gives me a once over, looking for injuries I'm sure.

"Never better." Offering him a small smile in gratitude, I turn to look at the barrier we created around us. "It'll take a lot more than Colt to mess me up." Watching him from the corner of my eye, I smirk. "I survived an encounter with an Archangel and a bunch of fallen. A whelp has nothing on me."

His shoulders shake with his chuckle. "I know you don't want us mentioning him, but you have so much of your father in you."

"I came to terms with it, Beelzebub. You can talk about him as much as you like." At his skeptical expression, I laugh. "I like to think I have just as much of my mother, too. So, I can't be all bad, right?"

"You have more of your mother than you may think." That got my full attention. "Sedakiel might be an Archangel of Mercy, but she is feistier than any other female I know." Humor twinkles in his red eyes when he grins at me.

"I like that."

"You've been very quiet and withdrawn since you woke up." Venturing consciously, he follows my example and scans the wards. "I know you don't trust us, and I don't hold it against you. I actually admire that about you. Trust should never be given; it should be earned. But if anything is wrong and you are not feeling well, we can help as much as you let us."

"I'll keep that in mind, but I'm good. I just need time to think." Shrugging nonchalantly, I push away the warm fuzzies his words gave me. Being accepted by the fallen was not on my bucket list, no matter how nice they are.

"Something has changed?" He keeps prodding.

Clutching the dagger tightly, my thumb rasps on the leather hilt. Ever since I woke up, I find myself holding it to keep me calm. "When I helped you seal the wards, it felt like some blockage was removed from me."

"What kind of blockage?" Noticing my reluctance, he lifts both palms in surrender. "I do not mean to pry. I'm only trying to see if I can help. Regardless of what anyone says, Satanael has been my brother since creation. You are his blood, and that's all that matters to me. Politics are Lucifer's problem. I couldn't care less."

"Even if that gives you an advantage?" Glancing at him slyly, I tell him without words he is full of shit. "Could've fooled me."

Laughter bounces off the walls, his large palms pressing on his chest. "You wound me." At my cheeky smile, he shakes his head. "You are more cunning than they give you credit for. I'm looking forward to seeing their faces when they finally realize it."

"Anywho…" Blowing out a breath, I ignore the easy way I can talk to Beelzebub. "After going kaboom"—I make an exploding motion with my fingers between us, enticing another chuckle—"something got unplugged. I feel whole now instead of like two people pushed inside one body."

"That is a good thing, no?"

"It feels that way, yes." Flinching when a massive demon with gray skin and four large horns hits the wards bursting into a puff of ash, I turn away from the courtyard. "I don't feel insane or evil, so it's good."

"If only horns and claws could give you a clear picture, life would be an easy journey. Evil has many faces Helena. You don't see it coming until it's too late." With those cryptic words, he walks away, leaving me watching after him.

His words keep repeating in my head as I wander aimlessly through the place. Not even the creepy clocks get my attention when I pass them heading for the room I've been given. It was where Eric and I stayed, although I haven't seen him since he made sure I'm fully awake. He kissed me senseless, crushing me to his chest like we'd never see each other again and said he would come back when he knew he was worthy.

Whatever that means.

I haven't felt his emotions, and while lost in my own troubles, I totally forgot to go look for him. With that thought pushing away Beelzebub's words, I square my shoulders, determined to knock some sense into Eric's stubborn head.

Chapter Twenty - One

"Where is Eric?" Barging in the room with the fireplace, which turned out to be Lucifer's favorite place to hang out, I zero in on him.

"Hello, Helena." Nodding as if I didn't almost rip his door off the hinges, he regards me calmly.

"Hello, Lucifer." Baring my teeth in a fake smile, I let it drop the same second. "Where is Eric?"

"How should I know? Sulking somewhere around here. We are all stuck, so he can't go anywhere, just like the rest of us." Frowning slightly, he even looks hurt. "He's been avoiding me and won't speak to me unless I'm willing to fight him," he admits begrudgingly.

"I wonder why," I tell him dryly.

"I believe Leviathan took him up on it." Blinking stupidly, it takes a moment for his words to register in my brain.

"Took him up on what exactly?" Dread pools in my stomach, remembering how Eric was clinging to me before storming out of the room.

"To fight." Swatting a hand like chasing a fly, his lips twist in a grimace.

"We must find him." Turning to go and do just that, I notice Lucifer is not following me. Storming back inside, I grab a fistful of his button-down shirt, yanking him to his feet. "Like now, Lucifer. He got himself in some shit, I just know it."

I race out of the door, dragging Lucifer along. He allows it obviously, or I wouldn't move him an inch, but I'm scared out of my mind for Eric not caring how he will react.

"I'll have you know, everyone else fears me." Drawling, he still keeps pace with me.

"I'll fear you too, but after we find Eric." Glancing over my shoulder, I nod at him. "Promise I will."

"You are a very peculiar creature." He keeps musing while I turn us through hallways.

The mention of a creature stabs me with guilt. After I woke up, I forced the Trowe to stay in the room. He refused adamantly at the beginning, but after threatening him that I would never allow him near me, he agreed begrudgingly to obey. Eric telling me that my sidekick stood up to Lucifer, protecting me when I crumbled on the ground, left me unnerved. I still haven't decided if having him around is a good or a bad thing.

"Yeah, I've heard that before, once or twice." After turning a corner on yet another hallway, I admit defeat. This place really is a maze created to confuse you enough to drive you insane. "I have no idea where I'm going."

"If you asked, I could've assisted you with directions." Sniffing like a snob, Lucifer smooths down the invisible wrinkles on his shirt.

"If you removed the stick that's so far up your ass, you would've heard that your son might be in danger." Spitting the words angrily at him, I vibrate with rage. The ground lurches beneath my feet, pushing us both on opposite sides.

Huffing superciliously, his gaze narrows at me. "It's only us here, the wards won't let anyone pass. He is safer than he's ever been. The only danger to him is his own anger and stubbornness."

"I wonder where he got that from." When his eyes turn to slits, I huff out a breath. "I'm not going to argue with you." Pressing fingers to my temples, I massage them in circular motion, hoping to elevate the budding headache. "I want to see with my own eyes that he is fine. Can you please lead the way?"

Without a word, he turns around, going back to where we came from. Clenching my teeth, I follow behind him, stewing in my anger. He would've let me walk around for days if I didn't say anything. What an arrogant jerk.

I keep telling myself that Lucifer is right. I saw it myself that nothing can get past the wards. No matter how many times I repeat it, the feeling that something is wrong keeps urging me to find Eric. Somewhere between the third, or was it the fifth, hallway, Beelzebub joins us, as well.

"Where are we headed?" Falling in step with me, he shoves his hands in his pockets.

"I'm looking for Eric, and Lucifer was kind enough to lead me to him."

"He left with Leviathan so they can release some aggression." Lucifer throws his words over his shoulder. "They are in the fighting arena."

"Umm…" Beelzebub starts walking faster. "I saw Leviathan fly out to scout the area a while ago."

Lucifer stops so suddenly my forehead bounces off his back. Beelzebub grabs my arm, preventing me from falling on my butt from the impact, and they exchange a weird look that curdles the blood in my veins. The next thing I know, Lucifer is bolting down the hallway like an arrow with Beelzebub and me at his heels.

"Where is Colt?" If that idiot did something to Eric, I'm seriously going to stab him in the forehead.

"Last time I saw him was when he left the palace." Beelzebub turns an intent look my way, reminding me he last saw Colt the same time I did.

"Colt is strong, but not strong enough to do any damage to Eric."

Lucifer doesn't even sound winded, while I'm breathing like a freight train. *Not unless Eric lets him do it.* I don't voice my fears, but they are there nonetheless, pushing me to run faster. The only thing stopping me from screaming his name like a crazy woman is the knowledge that I'm still in danger. As messed up as that sounds, I know at the bottom of my soul that he will never be far from me until I'm safe. Not for long anyway, and not if he can help it.

While my mind is giving me a pep talk, we reach a dead-end hallway with only one door at the far end. Made out of some silver metal—it could be real silver for all I know—it shimmers in the candlelight like a trap set up for unsuspecting passersby. Without slowing down, Lucifer bursts through it, the heavy door slamming open and staying embedded in the wall. Beelzebub is next behind him, and I pass the threshold last.

Ending in a dead stop, I try to look at everything at once in hopes I'll see him. I expected a room, like the few I've seen in this place. This is like a totally different world. Lucifer was not joking or using the word in jest when he said arena. As long and as wide as two football fields, the center of the area is made out of packed dirt. All around, benches are layered in multiple levels, circling it and turning it into a ring.

My gaze lands on two creatures facing each other at

the center of it. A shiver passes through me when I notice two large piles on both sides of one of the demons made out of ripped limbs and other body parts. Thank god Eric is not here. The beast closer to us, with his back turned our way, has dark gray skin and claws as long as my fore-arm. They curl like snapping jaws of a beast every time he clenches his fist. My gut tightens at the sight. That's only until I take a good look at the other one.

Dark gray skin makes him almost appear like he is made out of smoke. Amber eyes are blazing with unre-strained fury while his large body twitches as if preparing to pounce. He has two sets of horns, smaller ones curling up from the far sides of his forehead and large ones like a minotaur shooting up from his temples. Mused up hair tangles around them, giving him even more of a wild appearance. High cheekbones stretch his skin, sharp enough to cut if you touch them. To my horror, I find him as handsome as he is terrifying. Disturbed by that last bit, I turn to Lucifer.

"We must've missed him. I'm sure he went back to our room." Ignoring the fact my voice is shaky, I blow out a breath, acting like it's from all the running we did.

"What?" Lucifer looks at me like I'm nuts.

"Eric." Saying the name slowly in case his brain got damaged from the running, I swing my arm out, encom-passing everything around us. "He is not here."

"Get her out!" A voice that will haunt my nightmares

for as long as I live fills up the room. The sound deep and guttural, numbing my skull.

Too afraid of what I will see, I stare wide-eyed at Lucifer. His lips lift at the corners slowly, like the cat that ate the canary dropping my stomach at my feet.

"Of course, he is." Pointing a finger that I follow, my eyes lock on the rage-filled amber gaze of the beast.

"Eric?" At my timid whisper, the demon snarls before his furious roar shakes the walls around us.

Chapter Twenty-Two

There is a lot to be said about shock. In a split second, so many emotions slam inside you at once that at the end you feel absolutely nothing. Like an empty shell, all you can do is blink and hope that your heart eventually spatters to a start.

What have I gotten myself into?

That thought echoes in my head, bouncing around the empty cavern that is supposed to hold my brain like tumbleweeds in a deserted desert town. After an eternity of nothingness, an overwhelming need to get the hell out of here away from everyone and everything makes my muscles twitch, but my feet are rooted to the spot.

"I think she is in shock." Beelzebub bands down at the waist to peer at me.

Lucifer snorts.

Nothing could've worked better than that arrogance to snap me out of the state I'm in. Anger replaces all other emotion, and I grind my teeth at his gloating. The look on his face tells me that I've done something to please him immensely and that shit simply won't do.

Ignoring both of them, I focus on the demon. No, damn it, not a beast. Eric, I focus on Eric. No matter how he looks, it's still him down there under all the horns and claws. I have to believe that's true or I should use my own dagger and end my miserable existence. Squaring my shoulders, I lift my chin up and start down the endless stairs leading to the center of the arena.

"Get out!" Eric roars, rattling the benches, making me stumble a few steps before I straighten myself up.

"No!" Keeping my gaze locked on his, I continue moving down.

Panic flares in his eyes the closer I get, which looks hilarious on something as terrifying as him. The closer I get, the more comfortable it is to see the shadows swirling around him. Part of him, yet, separate. Everyone kept calling him Shadow, now I can see why that is. He looks like he is made out of shadows—solid shadows if there is such a thing.

When my boots hit the packed dirt, I'm still a good

ways away from him, but he takes a step back as if ready to run. Stabbing pain hits the center of my chest. Did he decide he doesn't want me to be his mate? As soon as the thought comes, I dismiss it. The way he was clinging to me the last time I saw him, the anguish in his eyes…it spoke of something else.

Recalling the conversation we had when we first got in this realm, it hits me that this has nothing to do with me. He thinks I would not accept him for who he is. The whole bullshit story he gave mc after I was rescued, keeping things from me that seemed a ridiculous thing to omit, hinting he is not worthy. All that because of his fear that I will not accept who he really is.

He was not far off in the assumption he made the first night I met him. I would've killed him, or at least tried to, the first chance I got. But that Helena, and this one now striding towards a seven-and-a-half-foot demon in the middle of Hell while two fallen angels watch, are two different people.

Passing the other demon, I realize it's Colt. He is already back to looking like himself, the creepy long claws nowhere in sight. Ignoring his stupid ass, I keep walking towards Eric. I know if I look away and break eye contact he will be out of here so fast it'll take me days until I find him in this maze of hallways. His muscles tighten like he is ready to bolt.

"If you take one step from where you are standing, I

swear to everything I hold dear I'm going to stab you in the nose, Eric." A choking sound comes from somewhere behind me, sounding suspiciously like Beelzebub trying to cover a laugh.

"Get out!" The shadows darken around him, sneaking on the ground and snapping like chihuahuas at my ankles.

"Or what?" Not slowing even for a second, I keep advancing on him. "What are you going to do, huh?"

"I don't want you, Helena. You need to leave, go home." His clawed fists clench at his sides. "This is where I belong." Rage burns in his glowing amber eyes when he takes a threatening step towards me. "This is what I am."

"I know who you are dumbass. I was there when I met you. Does being what you are come with a second set of horns or are they optional?" This time, Beelzebub does laugh, the sound giving me the strength to continue. "I can see the advantage."

"Get out, Helena!" He takes another step closer, and the temperature around us rises to an uncomfortable level.

Hatred blazes in the amber orbs that are focused entirely on me. Good thing too, because I'm close enough now to smell the stench of blood, sweat, and dirt coming off of the dismembered bodies stacked in piles on both sides of Eric. Him lashing out to protect himself emotionally I can handle. God knows I've done it enough to recognize it for what it is. Sadness makes tears prickle my eyes, but I blink them away. If he sees pity, I might lose him forever. Tantrums I can handle.

"You wanna deal with this here? Like this?" Tilting my head, I size him up.

Eric is bigger than me in normal circumstances, and changed like this, he can crush me like a bug with one hand. I'll have to use my smaller size to my advantage, praying to anyone that listens that we will walk out of this with no regrets and better for it. I might've had my misgivings before, but after expending my energy to the point of no return and surviving it, I see things differently. Hell, I'm different since I woke up. It's time to show Eric just that. Bouncing on the balls of my feet, shaking my arms like a boxer before a match and rolling my neck, I grin at him. His eyes widen for a second.

"Playtime jackass."

Not giving him time to think, I close the distance between us in a sprint. Catapulting myself as high as I can, I push off his chest with one foot, sending the other flying at his head in a perfect round kick. With a backflip, I end up on my toes facing him. He falls back but lifts up faster than I like, shaking his head to clear it. He is not even fully standing when he launches at me, his giant claw-tipped hands reaching to grab me. Pivoting out of his reach, my boot slams at the back of his knee, sending him faceplanting in the dirt.

"Aww, look at that. This is what I am." Mimicking his deep, gravelly voice, I taunt him.

And I shouldn't have done that.

He doesn't want to hurt me, I know that without a

doubt, but I'm also aware that the chain of clusterfucks has pushed him to the edge. With a roar, he moves so fast I only see a blur of gray stripes, and the next thing I know, my back hits the unforgiving ground, forcing all the air from my lungs out. A crunch tells me at least one rib is cracked or broken, and stars dance in front of my eyes.

When my vision clears, and I'm not gasping, I blink into clarity the worried face looming above me. Eric is still in his demonic form, but the shadows seem lighter, like they are struggling to hold onto their shape. Clenching my jaw and bracing for the pain, I jackknife my legs, trapping his ankles and sending him crashing to the ground next to me. Rolling on top of him, I press my dagger under his chin.

"The big bad demon fell for the oldest trick in the book." I don't sound as cocky as I would've liked when I wince from the sharp pain in my ribs, but whatever. He gets the point I hope.

"Hel?" He is searching my eyes, and I let him see how much I care. That I know exactly what he is doing, and no matter what, I'm not going anywhere. How much it hurts me to see him pushing me away. The demon under my thighs gradually gives way to my Eric.

"You know humans have this thing called communication. It solves a lot of unnecessary problems. You should try it sometimes." Removing the dagger and sliding it back into the small of my back, I give him a lopsided smile. And then I hit him one last time.

The sound of the slap is like a gun going off in the silent arena.

My palm is tingling from the force of the hit, but the look on Eric's face is priceless. When he turns his face back to me, those deep green eyes are shimmering with unshed tears, and I'll never tell him that I saw it. I will cherish seeing that emotion for the rest of my life and remember it in moments when he tests my patience. It seems all of us are dealing with emotional issues, no matter what species we are.

"Don't you ever do that to me again, Eric! We good?" I hold my breath until he nods.

Folding my body over his, I wiggle my head between his shoulder and neck, inhaling his scent. My body lifts up with the amount of air he drags in before he sighs, his arms closing around me.

"We shall leave them be." Lucifer's voice floats to my ears. "They know where to find us."

Their footsteps grow fainter before disappearing completely, leaving us alone, laying between piles or ripped up demons. Not the romantic setting I would prefer, especially with my ribs smarting, but I'll take it. The way my life is going, who knows? Maybe this is the best romantic setting ever when your mate is the Prince of Hell, his father is Lucifer, and you are apparently Satan's daughter.

"Yeah," Eric kisses the top of my head. "We are good. I'm sorry, Hel."

I think I mumbled he should stop apologizing, but I can't be sure it wasn't just in my head. I feel suddenly so tired the darkness claims me from one thought to the next.

Chapter Twenty-Three

Eric

"If you don't back off, I'll skin you." Snapping at the Haltija, I keep my voice low not to wake Helena.

The damn thing has been whimpering and pulling his hair out in fistfuls ever since I brought her to our room. I'm not sure if he thought she was dead, or if the smell of blood, dust, and a dead demon got him into a frenzy. I had to restrain him after placing her on the bed when he tried to crawl in there with her.

I might be an asshole for not talking things through with her, and for trying to get her to hate me, but I'll be damned if I let anyone in bed with her. The Trowe is more like a pet than a male, but that's beside the point.

"You let her get hurt, Shadow." Hissing at me, he claws the blankets at the foot of the bed. "I will sip your soul slowly if she doesn't wake up."

Feeling Helena stir next to me, I look at the Trowe contemplatively. "She is fine, just needs rest." Baring his teeth, he keeps pulling his hair in clumps. "But if you want to punish the one that hurt her, I can tell you who it was."

"It was you. I know it." But doubt is plastered over his wrinkled face.

"Okay, I won't tell you. I'll go punish them myself after I'm sure she is healed and well."

"Who?" Grabbing my arm, he yanks on it. "Who was it, Shadow?"

Pretending to be angry, I fling him off me. "If was Colt. The bastard will pay when I get my hands on him."

"I will make him pay, Shadow." Jumping off the floor where I pushed him, he bolts for the door. "You look after the mistress." The door closes with a bang, and I bite my lips not to laugh.

"You're such an asshole." Chuckling, Helena turns to me.

"He was throwing hair everywhere and annoying the shit out of me." Pushing the hair off her face, I smile at her. "Colt deserves to deal with it."

"What's his problem anyway?" Stretching her arms

and legs, she tests the stiffness of her limbs, nodding appreciatively when she realizes she's not in pain. "I'm guessing this is your doing?"

"As much as I want to take credit for it, and the fates know I can use anything I can to my advantage after the shitty move I pulled, you healed on your own." Laying on my back next to her, I stare at the ceiling. "Hel, I'm not sure what to say. You didn't deserve to be treated the way I treated you."

"No, I didn't." Her voice is level and calm.

Sighing, I close my eyes, wishing I was better with words. "You deserve to know the truth. To make your own mind up whether you find me repulsive or not."

"Yes, I do deserve that." Not a hint of how she feels about it can be heard in the tone of her voice.

"If I stayed here, I must punish those that have tainted their souls. You see, what my father said was the truth, but not the whole truth. They really are not fallen from grace. They are tasked to rule their domains. Taunting and tempting the humans is part of that. When the human succumbs, their souls are tainted. When they finally come here, they will have to face me. I'm their shadow self. Everything they hate about themselves, everything they fear or are ashamed of…I show them that. Not just physically torturing them until they pay their penance, but mentally as well."

Helena says nothing. I decide to push through this and get it out in the open once and for all. Swallowing thickly,

I clench my fists and brace myself for whatever reaction she is going to have.

"He trained me for it by showing me how it needs to be done. By doing it to me for a century until he was certain I was ready." The beast inside me is still close to the surface, and I feel my claws lengthening and piercing the skin on my palms. "What you saw in there, Hel, that's what I am." Her small hand wraps around my fist, and it startles me out of the dark memories clouding my mind.

"You didn't hurt me." Her soft words are gentle, and guilt shreds my black heart.

"I was that beast for a long time." Determined to get it all out, I continue ignoring the hope her words are trying to give me. "This male you see, the one you know was nowhere in sight. I was mindless, cruel, merciless, just like my father. So, beyond the edge of sanity that he used to keep me restrained, chains spelled by his powers, holding me back from ripping everyone apart. Be it in this realm…or any other."

Letting the silence stretch between us, those days flip in my mind's eye like a horror movie come to life. The rush and euphoria bubble in my veins, the alluring song of power calling no matter what I do to ignore it and pretend it's not there.

"Maddison was the only one that would survive to be near me. She is the one that brought me back long enough to take me to the human realm with her. When my father found me gone, he was furious. Lilith promised me that I would not be kept here if I come to face him one last time. To tell him I'm staying in the human realm."

"It's when you lost your wings." Propping on her elbow, she finally looks at me, but I keep staring at the ceiling.

"It wasn't a bad trade, Hel. Without the wings, it felt like part of me was missing, but it was much easier to keep the beast locked deep enough inside to pretend I'm something else."

"You keep saying beast. There is no one else inside you but yourself, Eric."

"I know that now." Grinding my teeth, I can hear the sound of bone scraping loud in my ears.

"You know shit." Placing her hand on my face, she turns my head so I have to look at her. Anger blazes in her green eyes, shocking me enough that all I can do is stare at her. "Whatever he said and did to you was his way of making sure you can do your duty. Was it a good thing to do? No. Was it necessary? How do we know? I was shitless scared of your father. As stupid as it may be, I thought that just seeing him or being in his presence would make me evil. Because no matter what kind of a beast you are, I'm still the hybrid. An abomination."

"You are not…" She places a hand over my mouth.

"Hector hired you to kill me, remember?" She searches my gaze. "The man that raised me and made me who I am looked specifically for you to be the one to end my life. Don't you find that strange? If anyone would know what kind of mindless beast you are, I'd think it would be Hector. Or maybe God, fates, or whatever you want to call it, has a screwed-up sense of humor putting us together like this?"

Removing her hand from my lips, I kiss the center of her palm before setting it on my chest. "Where did this come from?"

"Ever since I woke up, I've been thinking about it. I keep replaying every detail from the moment that rogue raked its claws on my arm. The more I think about it, the more everything looks planned. Like every moment, encounter, and problem is carefully planned to lead us to something. Even when other things seem most important, we get sidetracked and pushed in a different direction."

"What are you saying, Hel?" Everything she says slowly starts making sense, moving pieces of the puzzle around and putting them together.

"When I think about all the choices we've made so far, I came to one conclusion. There was never a choice, Eric. It seemed we made a choice one way or another, but when you look at the bigger picture, they were made for us. We just followed along blindly under the assumption that we had no other option." My chest swells when I see determination set on her beautiful face, her hair falling around us like a curtain. "I decided not to play the game anymore."

"I'm not sure that's an option, Hel."

"The way I see things it is. We are both being used.

They manipulate us, yet, we are still alive. But, earlier in that arena, I realized one thing. I almost lost you." Unshed tears gather at the corners of her eyes, and I feel sucker-punched in the gut. "Beast or not, it is you. Only you. And you are the only thing keeping me grounded in this crazy world I find myself in. Even feral you didn't hurt me, Eric. You lashed out, yes but didn't really hurt me. You came back from that mindless state like I knew you would. And that, to me, means everything. You have killed? So have I. I'm a hunter if you forgot. I finally saw the gray you were talking about. I know that not everything is black and white. And I accept both. You and that beast, because you are one and the same. At least to me."

"I don't deserve you." Voice thick with emotion, my hands tremble when I take her face between them.

"You don't, but you're stuck with me nonetheless." Her lips press to mine gently. I roll on top of her, pushing my tongue past them and tangling it with hers.

Chapter Twenty-Four

Helena

The taste of Eric overwhelms my senses. Caged between his arms, I sink into the thick mattress, surrendering to the pent-up tension that's been festering inside me every time he even looks at me. His tongue glides around mine in slow, sensual strokes, caressing the fire in my lower belly. I can tell that he is holding back, his body trembling beneath my fingers, while I'm clawing at his back.

Pulling back, we come up for air. I chase his lips, but he keeps just out of reach, frustrating me enough that a growl reverberates through my chest. The hunger in his eyes is tinged with hesitation, vivid enough that my brain gets out of the gutter, enough to function sufficiently. He is still unsure of how I feel about him after seeing him in his true form.

"I want you, Eric." Tracing his lips with my thumb, I hold his gaze. "I will always want you, horns and all. Just never change who you are in your heart."

Those words unleashed the beast. The human-looking one I've missed more than I was aware of. He kisses me wildly, our teeth clashing, the taste of blood mingling with our tongues. Frustrated that after all the time I've begged him to find a shirt and is finally wearing one now, I claw at the fabric. Chuckling in my mouth, he lifts slightly, helping me to pull it over his head.

When his skin touches mine, I moan low and long, spurring him on to rip at my shirt. With open-mouthed kisses, he travels down my neck and shoulder, nipping at the skin where they meet. His calloused fingers lift the weight of my breast, leading the stiff nipple to his waiting mouth. When he swirls his tongue around it, my back arches off the bed. He closes his teeth on the hard peek, lashing it with his tongue while his other hand glides over my shoulder and back, wrapping around my hip and pulling me roughly to him.

The sounds I'm making should embarrass me, but I'm too far gone to care even if Lucifer himself is standing just outside the closed door. Eric's appreciative grunts and moans only feed my mindless need while my legs shift restlessly between the sheets.

"Off." I'm pleading more than demanding, but I don't care. "Take everything off now."

"I thought you'd never ask."

Grunting, he releases my breast and starts tugging my pants over my hips. Lifting my butt off the bed, I help him as much as I can, my fingers yanking on the buttons of his pants. Impatient, he jerks mine down in one move, throwing them somewhere to the side. My panties are not so lucky when he rips them off me with both hands, his upper lip lifting over his teeth like a snarl. It would've looked terrifying if I wasn't snarling myself while unsuccessfully trying to get him as naked as I was.

Jumping off the bed, he drops the damn things at his feet, showing that he was commando under the dark denim. His thick erection springs up, pointing at his belly button, and I squeeze my thighs to elevate the pressure building there. Eric will have none of that.

Grabbing my ankles, he pulls my legs apart, dropping on his knees and wedging his broad shoulders between them. Sliding both his hands under my ass, he yanks me closer to the edge of the bed, and his mouth latches on my center none too gently. Twisting a handful of sheets in my fists, my mouth opens in a silent scream when I feel his wet tongue lap at my folds. His fingers tighten on my ass, tilting my hips up before he spears the tongue inside my channel. I almost lift off the bed, my back arching like a bridge. Releasing the sheets, my fingers tangle in his hair, holding him where I want him as if he was trying to escape.

The sound he makes, between a groan and a moan, sends a current up my spine and I'm horrified when wetness starts gushing out of me, drenching his face. When I try to pull away, he holds me tighter, and what I found embarrassing only makes him crazed. His teeth close around my clit when two of his fingers slide inside me, ripping a scream from my chest. He curls them up, pumping them fast while the tip of his tongue stimulates me relentlessly. My hips are diluting wildly with a mind of their own while my fingers find their way to tangle in his hair. Shamelessly, I keep riding his face while he is making growling sounds like the beast he keeps calling himself.

Eric doesn't let me come down from the mind-boggling feeling that he brought me to. His fingers keep pumping, the tips hitting that spot inside me that turns me into a beast as well. The pressure keeps building inside me, reaching a level that borders on pleasure and pain. It's too much too soon. The rubber band keeps tightening, my thighs quivering around his shoulders, but he keeps going. My eyes roll to the back of my head a moment before the pressure reaches its peak, and with a piercing scream that probably even the Holy ass can hear up in Heaven, I cum so hard that darkness takes me for a staggering moment before dumping me with a jolt back in my body.

Eric removes his fingers, wrapping his lips around them and cleaning them up with a twirl of his tongue. His eyes are blazing when they lock on my half-lidded gaze, and new heat gathers in my belly. Crawling up my body like a feline, his lips curl at the corners in arrogant male pride, and before I can see what he is planning, he slams himself inside me so hard I can feel the mushroomed head hitting my womb. A pathetic moan is all I can manage.

With his arms wrapped around my back, he lifts me up and moves us to the center of the bed, still as deep inside me as he can possibly get. I cling to him weakly, still not fully recovered from the shattering orgasm I experienced a few seconds ago. He spreads his thighs wider, pushing my legs further apart as he wraps both his hands around my hips in a tight grip.

"Hold onto the headboard, Hel." Panting and flexing his fingers on my hips, he snarls at me. "Do it now."

My arms lift like he controls them with his words and my fingers slide under the solid headboard. The moment my nails press to the wood, Eric starts pumping his hips at a punishing tempo. I realize this moment how much it cost him to hold back so he can give me pleasure first, and a blast of warmth spreads through my chest. He looks terrifying and so beautiful with his jaw set and eyes squinted while he chases his pleasure that the rubber band in my belly starts tightening again. His thickness stretches my channel to its limits, making it impossible not to feel him being a part of me. Like he is branding me, in case I forget who I belong to. And as strange and as unbelievable as it may sound, I don't mind it at all. Something in me purrs at the fact he wants to mark me.

Removing my hands from the headboard, I grab hold of his forearms. I'm not sure what that means to him instinctively, but both sets of horns start growing on his head. His features sharpen, the color of his skin darkening. He hunches his body over mine, and fascinated, I reach up, wrapping my fingers around the more extensive set curling up from his temples. The heat in the room skyrockets. Even the temperature of his erection that keeps pumping inside me goes up, warming my insides and adding to the frenzy we are both in. Tightening my legs around his thighs, I start meeting every pump of his hips. Eric starts growling in that deep guttural voice, and the tightening inside me snaps without warning.

Screaming his name, I shatter around his thickness a second before he roars my name loud enough to make my ears ring. Hot jets splash my insides, and they keep going long enough to begin leaking out, drenching us where we are joined. Colors swirl behind my closed eyelids and just when I think it's over, Eric's sharp teeth sink into my shoulder, drawing blood. Another mind-blowing orgasm hits me, and as soon as I come down from the height, I pass out.

Chapter Twenty-Five

I feel like a wet noodle. Languidly stretching my arms above my head, I can't stop the stupid smile that makes my cheeks hurt. Holy shit. We've had sex before, but what happened today was enough to scare the crap out of me and make me giddy to experience it again at the same time. My smile grows when Eric starts placing kisses wherever he can find skin. Giggling like an idiot, I finally open my eyes to look at him.

"You've been holding out on me." Nudging him with my hip, I'm happy to see we are both still gloriously naked.

"Only you would say that after a beast was rooting on

you like he's deprived." Snorting, he shakes his head, but his eyes are twinkling.

"It's my beast, so he can root anytime he likes." Shrugging nonchalantly, I squeal when he tickles me. "Hey! Cut it out."

"I love seeing you smile and laugh."

"I know you do." Spearing my fingers through his hair, he groans, closing his eyes when I scratch his skull with my nails. "You also love it when I kick someone's ass or when I shoot you, too. So that's not saying much. You know that, right?"

A whispering sound is all the warning we get before a wrinkled face with a couple of patches of missing hair plops above us on the bed. With a shriek, I kick out with my leg, sending the Trowe flying and hitting the wall next to the partially open door.

"Oh my God." Hastily wrapping the sheets around me, I lift up on my knees, hiding behind Eric. "Are you fucking insane? I'm naked! Get the hell out!"

Eric is shaking, so I wrap one arm around him to hold him back from killing my sidekick while clutching the sheets with the other at my chest. The Trowe lifts off the floor with a look of a kicked puppy, minus the eyes, since he doesn't have any, and guilt tries to eat me alive. That's until I peer at Eric and see that he is not shaking in anger or because he is holding himself back from killing the Trowe.

"Are you laughing?" My voice is shrill, and I stare at

him incredulously. "You really are an asshole, you know that? I'm naked! Hello!"

"Sorry mistress," the damn Trowe hisses, still standing sadly at the door.

"You should be. You need to knock, that's why there is a door there." Turning to the asshole next to me, who is still laughing by the way, I jab a finger at him. "A door that should've been locked."

"I was a little preoccupied to think of the door." Shrugging unapologetically, he grins at me.

The door opens again.

"Yes, we all heard that you were preoccupied." Beelzebub waltzes inside and I gape at him for a second.

"Out!" Grabbing the pillow next to me, I chuck it in his face. "Get out!"

The pillow hits Beelzebub square in the face and bounces off him, dropping at the feet of the Trowe. The creepy bugger picks it up and, burying his face in it, starts sniffing loud lungfuls of air.

"Eww, stop that!" Rubbing my face in frustration, I almost drop the sheets. "Oh, my God, this is so not happening to me right now."

"Looking for Him in Hell. Now that really is something." Beelzebub chuckles. Groaning, I thump my forehead on Eric's back. "If you are wondering why Eric is not feral and trying to kill us with both of us being male"—Hitching a thumb at the Trowe he grins—"and here while you are naked. It's because he left his permanent mark on you. Any male within a few miles radius will know now they'll have to go through him if they want to have you." He nods approvingly at Eric. "Well done."

"This is so not happening." Mumbling, I can't even find it in me to argue anymore.

"You needed something?" Eric is obviously done laughing.

"Leviathan never returned." A frown pulls his brows slightly over his eyes. "And we can't find Colt."

"I looked for him, as well," the Trowe hisses angrily, thankfully done with sniffing the pillow. "I lost his trace at the gates. It's where his scent ends."

"That's impossible!" Beelzebub glares at the Trowe. "Even we can't leave the wards. I know, because I tried. We are all stuck here unless we remove them."

"Then how did Leviathan leave?" Eric and Beelzebub look at me sharply, and I bristle. "What? It's logic, no? If none of us can leave, how did he end up going wherever?"

"Maybe only through the air?" Beelzebub doesn't believe his own words judging by the puzzled look on his face.

"That's easy to check." Pushing on Eric's shoulders, I shuffle on my knees to get off the bed.

"How?" Eric is the one asking, and I almost laugh.

"Did you lose your brain, or do you need time to recover?" When he scowls at me, I do laugh. "You'll fly dumbass. Let me get dressed, and we will test it."

"I keep forgetting they are back." Stretching his shoulders, he goes looking for his own clothes, undisturbed that all of us can see his naked ass. It's a very nice ass, but still. No one cares about modesty here.

Beelzebub left to wait in the hallway with the Trowe, so I dress quickly, and we head for the courtyard. Eric skipped a shirt since he will be our lab rat, and my face burns when memories of the last couple of hours flood my mind. Butterflies unfurl in my belly, and I stiffen when three pairs of nostrils flare up in a long sniff.

"I have my dagger on me and if anyone says a word, I'm going to stab them."

They chuckle, but lucky for them no one says anything. I was not joking that someone was going to end up a shish kabab if they even opened their mouth. When we finally reach the courtyard, Lucifer is already waiting for us. He doesn't say anything either, but he doesn't have to. A satisfied smile is curling his lips, like me and Eric fucking was done for his personal pleasure. Anger sparks inside my chest, but I push it down. Now is not the time to deal with this. We have bigger problems if the wards are messed up.

"Okay, let's try it." Eric takes a step away from me, but I stop him.

"Wait." Turning to Beelzebub, I stab a finger at the gates. "Try them first to see if they are working. They've left, maybe enough of them turned to ash that we can try removing them now." No more demons are snarling and throwing themselves at the wards. That must be a good sign.

Beelzebub gives me a skeptical look, but he walks up to the gates, jamming both his hands into the barrier that we erected with the wards. A blast of energy hits him like a punch to the chest, sending sparks everywhere. Thankfully he doesn't turn to ash, but he does get thrown all the way back, hitting the walls of Lucifer's home.

"They are working." With a groan, he lifts himself up, glaring at me.

"It was worth a try." Shrugging a shoulder, I bite on my lip so I don't laugh at how disheveled he looks.

Eric takes a few steps away from us, and his wings unfurl from his back. My lips part in silent awe at how beautiful they are. He gives me a lopsided smile, the green darkening in his eyes, before he pushes off the ground with one powerful beat of the wings. Dust puffs up in small clouds around us, and I watch him go, moving higher in the air. When he reaches the tops of the highest towers, he slows down, lingering there for a moment. Looking down at me, I give him an encouraging nod and a thumbs up.

"Lucifer if he starts going down and you don't catch him, whatever you are hoping I will help you with will never happen. I'll die before I do anything for you if he gets hurt."

"Duly noted," he murmurs, not denying that he has an agenda for being so accommodating.

Eric looks up at the sky before sweeping his wings in one hard push and catapulting himself at the barrier. I brace for the impact, poising my body to spring and try to catch him if he starts falling in case Lucifer decides to be an ass. I shouldn't have worried because he goes through it.

"Huh." Relaxing, I blow a loud breath through pursed lips. "Maybe it's not like a dome? We didn't cover the top?"

"Wc did."

Lucifer is frowning, and the doubtful look on his face gives me an idea. Spinning on my heel, I stride to the gates and push my hands through the wards without stopping, or I'll change my mind. Braced for the blast, my eyes are squeezed shut but the pain never comes. When I peel one eyelid open, I see the hands are through the wards.

"Maybe not all of us are stuck?" Looking over my shoulder at Lucifer, I see him walking determinedly towards me.

A dark shadow falls over him, and I lift my face up with a smile, expecting Eric to be coming down. My smile is left frozen on my face when I see Leviathan in his dragon form snatching Eric in his outstretched claws. A scream is ripped from my chest when one of the claws slides between Eric's ribs, and he goes limp.

Chapter Twenty-Six

Lucifer doesn't wait for me to say anything. I'm assuming the look on my face is enough to speak volumes, leaving me grateful when black wings spring from his back almost twice the size of the ones Eric has. Without turning, he flings himself in the air, sending my hair over my face by doing so. Hurriedly, I move the mane away from my eyes to see what's going on just in time to watch the dragon lift his humongous head up and belch a stream of fire in the sky, bathing it in flames.

My heart lurches in my chest, worry eating me alive that there is nothing I can do for Eric.

When we finally work through the hurdle standing between us, this monster will take him from me. Horrified, I watch Lucifer hit the wards in the air and start falling down, spiraling out of control. Another burst of flames turns everything around us red, the fire burning bright above us longer than any natural occurrence will. Leviathan continues to shake his head from left to right, and back again, like some serpent on crack feeding the raging inferno.

"Beelzebub!"

Screaming from the top of my lungs to be heard over the crackling sound of flames and a furious dragon, I point at the still falling Lucifer. How ironic for the first fallen angel to be falling again in the middle of Hell. To my horror, Beelzebub only shakes his head, jabbing his finger in the same direction. He turns his back on me and, sprinting to the wall closest to him, starts climbing the smooth surface, his claws digging holes and raining pebbles on the ground.

Knowing no help will come from him, I bolt in the direction of Lucifer's fall. If nothing else, I'll soften the hit with my own body, giving him a faster recovery time. I can't fly, so he is my only hope that Eric can be saved from the pissed off dragon.

If he is still alive, a snide voice chirps in my head, numbing me with fear.

A gust of hot air is pushed my way, causing the sweat from the heat to run like raindrops down my face and back. Looking up with squinting eyes, I see Lucifer has leveled himself a few feet away from the ground. Hope surges through me that we can still have Eric back before it's too late.

"I can't get past the wards." Shaking his head to clear it, Lucifer focuses his intent gaze on mine. "Come!"

Closing the distance between us, he reaches for me, and without a second thought, I grab his outstretched arms, letting him swing me up in the air. The Trowe screams something in the background, but I don't have it in me to worry about the sidekick now. He can deal with his clinginess on his own. Wrapping myself around Lucifer's torso like a monkey, I cling to him when he takes me up again, leading us closer to Eric.

I've been this close to Lucifer when he tried to kill Eric, but he was pissed off at the time, and his powers were almost burning my skin. I'm surprised that at the moment, even when he changed his somewhat human appearance, it doesn't feel as uncomfortable as I expected it to be. Isn't he as pissed off that the one he trusted is trying to kill his son? Why does his power feel tempting, alluring, almost inviting me to press myself closer? Bile rises in my throat when my lower belly tightens from our proximity. Sinful thoughts cloud my mind, my legs tightening around his narrow waist.

"We can't get to him if I can't go past the wards, Helena," Lucifer murmurs in my ear, covering my arms in goosebumps. "I will need your blood if we are to save him."

Panic hits me like a slap in the face, overriding whatever it is that's wrong with me right now. Alarms are blaring in my head, telling me all this is just an elaborate trick to help him reach the end game he's been playing this whole time. My gaze swings up, searching for my mate. He is still dangling lifelessly in one of Leviathan's claws like a broken doll clutched in a petulant child's hand. His beautiful wings are draped around him, drops of blood dripping from the one closest to the pierced ribs and the deadly claw.

Heart jackhammering in my chest, I look for Beelzebub, praying he is closer to reaching the top behind the dragon. Rocks and dust rain down the smooth walls while he moves faster than I thought possible up the walls. He still won't make it time if the continuous blasts of fire are any indication.

Did it all come to this? I wonder. Is this some sort of a cosmic joke that I will survive this long, fight with everything in me to keep my life, to push past my beliefs and convictions to find love with a man that represents everything I stood against just so I have to choose to either save him or those poor souls in my realm that know nothing better? And all for what? For my selfish desire to keep breathing while Heaven and Hell have no qualms about killing to get to my blood?

What exactly were my parents thinking, creating an abomination such as myself? Did immortality bore them so much that they simply created an entertainment to keep things interesting among these powerful entities that prove they place no value on human life? Numbness settles like a heavy anvil around my ankles. They care nothing about me or even Eric. We are just toys, scattered around to fill their endless time when the thought strikes them. Only to kick us aside or throw us away when they get bored again.

It's all games.

"It is okay, Helena." Lucifer rubs my back with one of his hands soothingly. "I know you don't trust me, and I do not blame you for that. If we can't save Eric, there is still Colt. He might be rough around the edges, but he can be brought under control."

"What?" Startled by his words, I gape at him, stupefied. "Did you just try to pimp out your other son in case the man I love dies?"

"Don't be absurd." Looking down his nose at me, he seems insulted. Good! He damn well should be. "I know this is a tough decision to make. I'm only trying to soothe your fears."

"By telling me if Eric dies, it's okay because Colt is just there like some lady in waiting or something?" My fingers dig into his shoulders, making me wish I had claws as well so I can scratch his perfect, angelic face. "Listen to me and listen really good, asshole. You should be kissing Eric's feet and bowing to him." When he scowls at me, I nod to emphasize my words. "If it weren't for him, you would've had an army straight out of Heaven at your gates this very moment. So, before you dismiss him as you are obviously known to do, how about you think about that?"

Lucifer searches my face with a calculating look. Uneasiness crawls like icy fingers under my overheated skin and pouring sweat. This whole thing is so messed up it makes me dizzy. His face loses focus for a moment when a spell of lightheadedness hits me out of nowhere. Swaying in his arms, he tightens his hold around me when I almost slip from his grip.

Chapter Twenty-Seven

"Easy there, girl." Jostling me higher up his chest, he falters slightly in the air.

"There is nothing easy about this, Lucifer." Through clenched teeth, I push the words out without vomiting all over him.

"How much you care for him is admirable, Helena." Softening his dark eyes, he sighs, "As much as it pains me, unless you trust me enough to give me your blood, I'm afraid I'm powerless to stop whatever it is that's coming next." He points his chin above us.

With dread, I jerk my head up to look at Eric. My eyes are stinging from the blasting heat from the fires burning above our heads. Blinking away the tears that gather on my lashes, at first, I don't understand what Lucifer was pointing at. When my stinging gaze travels up the black body of the dragon, up his chest and neck, a scream pierces the air around us.

Leviathan is lowering his head down, his eyes large enough to be seen from this far burning with some crazed satisfaction at the look on my face. *No, no, no, no*, my mind chants as the large mouth full of razor-sharp teeth stretches in some ghoulish twisted smile, the forked tongue snaking out of it as if tasting my fear.

I'm not sure how I can notice anything else apart from my heart dying slowly in my chest at the scene unfolding in front of me. Lucifer's hand that was rubbing my back in soothing motions slowly inches lower, snapping me out of the horrifying state I'm in. Urgency moves my limbs faster than my brain can comprehend the action. I snatch my dagger from the small of my back where I had it tucked for safekeeping a second before his fingers brush the waistband of my pants. The dragon roars in rage, confirming my fears that this whole thing is some *Mortal Kombat* game we are all playing.

"Looking for this?" Sneering in Lucifer's face, I press the sharp blade under his chin. "You developed a nice tick in your jaw, I see." He glares, but I ignore it when a random thought hits me like a brick. *Tick.*

The clocks.

When we passed the hallway covered on all sides with clocks, they were all working. I have no idea why that didn't dawn on me as something important enough to mention at the time, but right now it's like a featured art piece in the middle of my head with all the light of the sun illuminating it. What happened that made them start working? Was it me and Eric? Did we trigger it somehow with our bonding, keeping in mind that Beelzebub said he fully claimed me permanently? Or is it something Lucifer did that started up this clusterfuck?

"Remove the dagger, Helena," he growls at me, icily. "Or he will die, along with everyone else."

"How about you tell your pet dragon to release him, and I'll think about it, huh?" Putting pressure on his neck, a smile starts forming on my lips when beads of blood coat the burnished metal.

If I was thinking rationally, I would've phrased my threat a hell of a lot better. Since I'm not, I watch with the breath stuck in my lungs when Lucifer smiles triumphantly at me before looking over my head at Leviathan. The Trowe screams from the ground, the sound alarmed like he is about to die himself. Torn between dreading to look at Eric's dangling body, checking on my sidekick, and not wanting to look away from the most significant threat that I hold captive with a dagger under his chin, panic pushes the anger I've buried in my chest to the surface.

No, not just anger, I realize, stunned. Anger and sadness mixed together, indistinguishable from one another. What kind of a pathetic existence all of them must have to resort to this? Trading the lives of their children to obtain the unobtainable ideal of their perceived victory. To be willing to die out of pride or greed for something that will never satisfy their insatiable hunger for more.

Golden light surrounds Lucifer and me. My body trembles in his arms, the force of my emotions pulsing from me in waves that I can't control. Flabbergasted, I watch Lucifer's movement's stop, his intent, furious gaze emptying out like his soul has left the shell behind. My stomach flip-flops, expecting us to plummet to the ground, but we stay up in the air. One strong pulse from my chest sends golden streaks striking through the sky in different directions, leaving me the only one able to move freely.

Twisting around in Lucifer's arms, I turn to check on Eric. A sharp pang of fear slams my ribcage when I see that Leviathan has released the hold and Eric is frozen in the air halfway to the unforgiving ground, still unconscious. *At least he stopped and is not falling.* The thought calms down my erratic fears.

The dragon is poised as if ready to strike at my turned back. His demonic sneer sending shivers up my spine while his outstretched claws are pointed in my direction. Just like Lucifer and Eric, he is surrounded by the golden glow turning him into a macabre 3D character that will star in all my nightmares if I survive this. He looks so eerie that even knowing he is unable to move, I'm reluctant to look away from him.

Unsure how much more time I have until everything comes back to life, I pull my gaze away to check on the Trowe. His scream still rings inside my head as vivid as if he is doing it right this moment. I find him just below me and Lucifer, his tiny body almost indistinguishable from this height. The wrinkled, eyeless face is turned up as if he was looking at me, but his small arm is pointing in the direction of the gates. I follow it and almost release my hold on Lucifer when I see the hordes of demons surrounding the place. They were not gone as my eyes told me, or they've come back while I was preoccupied with getting to my mate. Whatever happened, they were here now. All frozen, surrounded in a golden glow but not less terrifying.

Swallowing the lump of terror that stuck in my throat, I wonder how the hell did I get myself in this situation. Better yet, how the fuck am I going to get myself out of it? My mind spins, coming up with ideas and dismissing them the next second. Whatever I can think of, nothing seems possible for me, Eric, and my sidekick to get out of here in one piece. *And without giving your blood to Lucifer.* The smartass voice inside me finds it necessary to remind me; like I can forget such a thing.

My heart keeps slamming against my breastbone, the sound of my gasps of air echoing in my ears. I keep twisting and turning, looking from one disaster to another while unable to stay still, even if it means I'll drop from the frozen Lucifer statue. I mean, I froze them all like this, right? That means I should theoretically be able to unfreeze them.

Theoretically being the paramount term.

"I'm not sure we have time to keep staring at them if you want to get out of here." The deep voice makes me jump out of my skin, eliciting a shrill shriek from me that pierces the silence.

My grip on Lucifer slips, my sweaty hands sliding from his skin. I stare up at the still raging inferno above me, the fires turning the person that spoke into a menacing dark shadow while the air rushes past my ears, and I plummet down, gravity pulling me harder to my death.

Chapter Twenty-Eight

My hair flies up around my face like a banner, obscuring everything but the fire and the two dark shadows above me. The one on my left is Lucifer, still a floating statue, judging by the frozen state of his wings. The one on the right, however, doesn't stay there long. Like an arrow, the wings fold close to his back, and he closes the distance faster than I can blink. My neck almost snaps when my fall is jerked to a stop, and arms wrap around my knees and back.

"Let's not die yet, she-devil. I believe you have important things to do." Colt smirks at my stunned face.

"Why aren't you frozen?" Rubbing my neck, I wince at the stabbing pain from the whiplash he just gave me.

"I don't know." Shrugging, he slips back that annoying mask he wears all the time. "You like me, but you are not aware of it, yet?"

"Yeah, I wouldn't count on it, asshole. You can drop me now if that's your plan." Glaring at him, I tighten the grip on the dagger still clutched in my hand, making sure he sees it. "Your father tried that shit and look at what happened. You can join him if you like."

Colt twists his mouth like he tasted something horrible. "I'm not sure what is going on but that"—Tilting his chin up towards Lucifer, anger burns in his gaze—"is not my father. I noticed the difference when he walked you to the arena. That's why I went looking for answers."

"And I should just take your word for it?" I'm hoping he can see on my face how stupid I think his expectations are if that's the case. "You really think that's a jinn?"

"You have felt his power; do you really not notice the difference?" A slight frown forms between his eyebrows, reminding me so much of Eric my heart hurts.

Now hearing it said out loud, I know that my body warned me of the danger I was in, I was just too preoccupied to listen to it. Down here in Hell, my GPS is silent. I'm not sure if it's because of my powers finally snapping back in place, or because everything is evil so it doesn't know what to think. *Eric is not evil,* my mind reminds me.

"I noticed something different, yes. I just thought Lucifer was a jerk, as usual, trying to mess with my head." Flicking my eyes to check on Eric, I look back at

Colt. “It’s all a game to him. Can we get Eric now since you are so helpful for once?”

“I have to set you down first. I can’t carry you both at the same time.” Turning his body, he descends slowly, aiming for the place where the Trowe is standing.

“If you hurt him in any way, Colt…” I stare at him until he looks me in the eye. “I’m going to carve you up like a thanksgiving turkey so slowly, Hell will seem like Heaven compared to that. And this is a promise.”

“Got it.” Setting me on my feet gently, he takes a step away from me. “I’ll be right back.” He shoots up in the sky, leaving only a blast of air and a cloud of dust behind him.

Shading my eyes, I keep my gaze on him while inching closer to my sidekick. My knees buckle, and I barely stay standing when I see him take hold of Eric, and they begin to lower slowly. I’m guessing the extra weight is making Colt move slower than usual, going off his words and the speed he used to bring me to the ground. Assured Colt is keeping his word, I turn to the Trowe. A hysterical giggle comes out of my mouth when I see his twisted face. He froze while screaming whatever it was that he was trying to tell me, leaving him looking scary and hilarious at the same time.

Or, I’m just losing my mind.

“I’m sorry.” Not knowing what to do and feeling horrible for doing all the things so far to the poor bugger, I pat him awkwardly on the head.

As soon as my hand touches him, the golden light disappears. Oblivious to the time that has passed, his hissing shout, "misstresssssss, looookkkkkk," splits the air, followed by a scream coming from me. Jerking his head in my direction, the Trowe squeals again to which I join him.

"Stop yelling!" Pissed off that he freaked me out, I snap at him, and his mouth closes with a snap.

"What in the fates name is going on here?" Beelzebub's whispered yell makes me and my sidekick scream again like frightened little girls.

"Okay! The next one to scare me will die!" yelling with frustration, I brandish the dagger at all of them, including Colt, who is finally lowering Eric to the ground. "How are you not frozen as well?" Glaring at Beelzebub, I point my blade at him. "What the hell is happening?"

Jaw clenched and hands fisted at his sides, Beelzebub walks my way briskly. "I ducked."

"Excuse me?"

"What he said," Colt answers instead, finally standing up from his crouch over his brother. "That's how I'm still moving. I ducked, too, when you sent those projectiles out of your body." Shrugging, he folds his arms over his chest. "I thought you saw me and wanted to kill me if we are honest. I wasn't going to stand to test it out after our last encounter."

"I couldn't see where it came from, but I'm too fast when it comes to saving my hide." Grinning, Beelzebub rolls his neck. Seeing him move on those smooth walls, I believe his words without a doubt. He looked like the Tasmanian devil crawling up.

Ignoring them all, I drop on my knees next to Eric. My hand hovers above his body, but I'm too afraid to touch him in case he comes unfrozen. The hole from Leviathan's claw is wide enough that I can stick my hand in it, but that too is frozen, and no blood is coming out of the wound. That must be a good thing, right? Doubt gnaws at me, and I lift my gaze in question, looking between Beelzebub and Colt.

"Narsi got animated when I touched him." Using his name for the first time, I point at the Trowe to explain why I'm looking at them for answers. "I'm worried if I unfreeze Eric that he might die from the injury."

"I don't know what to tell you about that, but if we don't start moving, I think all of us will die from some type of injury." Beelzebub has a troubled expression on his face as he looks behind the gates.

"I don't know how long they'll stay like that." Chewing on my lip, I turn to glance at the angry, frozen horde of demons. The Trowe standing as close as he dares to me just adds to the creepy factor of the situation, especially when I can feel him breathing harshly in anticipation.

"We either run, or we fight." Colt glares daggers past the gates. "Or we barricade ourselves inside and hold the fort as much as we can." Glancing at me, he looks away fast when I notice the uncertainty in his eyes. All his assholeness is just an act, I realize.

So much like his twin brother.

"I'm not locking myself in here any longer." Squaring my shoulders, I steel my spine. "I need to get out of here and, most importantly, I need to close the gate that's been standing open—the one I opened—while we waste precious time here entertaining Lucifer and playing his twisted games." Grinding my teeth and praying for Eric to be okay, I reach for him again.

"Wait!" Beelzebub folds his large body, picking Eric up like he weighs nothing. "I'll carry him as much as I can. We can switch until he comes out of it on his own." Looking at Colt, he waits until the other nods to turn to me again. "If we are not staying here, I say we go now."

"And how will you pass the wards?" My neck hurts looking up at them, so I rub my hand over it.

"You'll drop the wards." My heart skips a beat at those words and Colt smirks. "We'll be ready to bolt as soon as it's done, in case they all come to at once."

"Don't you have wings, too?" Lifting off the ground, I dust my knees, glancing at Beelzebub. "Can't we just fly out of here?"

"Of course, I do." Looking insulted, he lets them burst out of his back. "Flying out is the plan, but we can't go on for a long time. The extra weight will slow us down. We got to gain some distance and walk from there."

"I'm not leaving Narsi." Snatching the Trowe's hand, I pull him to me.

"I'll carry you both. He weighs nothing." Colt comes next to me, and I force myself not to recoil from his touch now that my feet are on the ground. "He can climb on my back."

"Here goes nothing," I murmur when Colt scoops me up while my sidekick scrambles on his legs and wraps himself around like a backpack.

Chapter Twenty-Nine

Anticipation will eat me from the inside out. I can almost see the hole forming in my stomach while I chew through the skin on my thumb. Remembering all the chastising I used to get from my best friend about it, I lower my hand away from my teeth and almost laugh at the stupidity of the action. I neither have a best friend anymore, nor am I sure that I will live past this day to worry about anything else.

We lift in the air and stop right where I can see the shimmering in the sky where the wards form the barrier around us. The golden glow keeping everyone else frozen paints a clear picture of the monsters waiting to spring at us the second it disappears. Flicking my gaze from one snarling face to another is not helping my nerves one bit, so I decide to pretend they are not there. If I'm not looking at them, they'll disappear, right?

I wish!

"Ready?" Colt mumbles as if he doesn't want to disturb the already horrid silence.

"No." I lift my hands, contradicting my answer, bringing them in front of me palms facing the wards. "I need to get closer…I think."

What are you doing, Hel? That stupid voice in my head sounds incredulous and I know that it's right. I have absolutely no clue what I'm supposed to be doing to bring these suckers down. It's not like I knew what I did when we put them up in the first place. The thought occurred to me that I went kaboom and lost two days when I accidentally helped them shield us from the incoming horde, but I don't see how else we are going to leave this damn place. It was so much easier when others were making the decisions and all I did was follow orders. How ironic that not long ago I told Eric that we had no choices. Thinking of Eric pulls my eyes towards Beelzebub, hovering near us with my mate in his arms.

Lo and behold, Helena the demon hunter leaving her life and the life of the man she loves in the hands of two demons. All that while running away from an Archangel set up to kill her straight to the pits of Hell and Michael might not be an Archangel at all, but a jinn. My mind spins out of control, making me want to scream with this whole thing. It's so insane that I'm starting to hope that I'll wake up safe in my bed in Sanctuary and it'll all be just a terrible nightmare.

Only Sanctuary is not safe for me anymore, and I'm not a demon hunter either. I'm an abomination, the daughter of Satan himself. How's that for the twisted sense of humor by whoever orchestrates our lives? Anger replaces everything I feel at the injustice of it all. I never asked for any of this, yet here I am, paying for somebody else's mistakes. *Eric is paying, too,* my mind reminds me.

That golden glow that came from me earlier bursts through the center of my palms. The wards erupt like a light show blinding me for long moments before I blink everything into focus. When my eyes clear up, I gasp at the sight in front of me. Glancing at my companions, I see they are stunned as well. If I weren't so shocked myself, I would've laughed, especially at Beelzebub's face.

"Remind me of this next time I'm stupid enough to provoke her." Colt gulps loudly before turning wide-eyed at Beelzebub. The other nods a little too enthusiastically in answer.

Everything around us falls silent after the boom of the disintegrated wards. Not because everyone is still frozen, no. It's because whoever is left, they are looking in horror at the wide clearing my golden glow made in front of us. Every demon in its path is now piles of ash covering the dusty ground, small flakes still floating in the air like moths.

“Can we please get the hell out of here now?” hissing under my breath at Colt, I jab my elbow in his ribs, making him grunt. At least he snapped out of it.

“Let’s go.”

His sharp words pull Beelzebub out of his stupor, and Colt darts in the air so fast I have no other option but to press my face to his chest. Narsi squeals something from his back, but I can’t hear a word from the wind rushing at us at the speed we are going. And here I thought Colt moved slowly with added weight. The second he moves, his mighty wings so much like Eric’s beating the air with a vengeance, all hell breaks loose, literally.

“They have gorgons.” Beelzebub roars to be heard over the screeching and screaming of whatever is left from Mammon’s horde.

Cussing everything under the sun, using words I didn’t know existed and turning my ears red in the middle of Hell, Colt moves even faster, if that was possible. My skin feels like it’s being peeled off my body from the force of the air pelting us, and my sidekick wraps his fingers around my arms where I have them folded around Colt’s neck, giving me an extra hold no matter how deceptive it seems. If we continue at this speed, I’m going to fly out of the asshole’s arms any second now. A brain-numbing, furious screech sounds like it’s coming from right behind us and I do the impossible task of actually looking over Colt’s shoulder.

Female demons, two of them, with beastly features

and leathery wings like bats are flying at us with two sets of arms outstretched, their claws only inches away from the Trowe's back. Fear freezes my lungs, and with Narsi holding onto my arms, the speed we are moving makes it impossible to do anything but watch in horror when they snatch him away from us and toss him in the air like a useless rug.

My piercing scream makes Colt flinch, losing his grip on my body, and I follow my sidekick, flipping through the air the same way.

Chapter Thirty

The second time gravity tries to take my life, when no one else has succeeded, is when my life flashes in front of my eyes. Moments like my team sharing a meal joking and bickering among each other. Hector scolding me before patting me awkwardly on the shoulder, doing his best to hide the pride in his eyes. Amanda bumping her shoulder with mine, pointing her chin at some stupid thing George did while we snicker behind our hands. The day Hector gifted me my guns and the awe I felt when I held them in my hands the first time.

Eric.

His smirking face while we were fighting pressed back to back. The anguish in his eyes when Michael took me away. His beast glaring at me, hiding the vulnerability behind the terrifying shell. Closing my eyes, I hold on to the memory of his face with love shining in his beautiful green eyes. I will miss him terribly, but I will pray that he makes it out of here alive. My body slams into something, pushing all the air from my lungs with a loud *oomph*.

"You going to continue staying limp, or can you grab onto my neck?" Beelzebub growls over his shoulder.

Gasping to inflate my lungs with oxygen, I scramble around his broad back, careful not to grab his wings, wrapping around like an anaconda ready to strangle him. My limbs are shaking, the reality slamming into my brain that I almost splattered like a watermelon on the ground.

"Narsi!" My sidekick's name is a sob. "They tossed him off Colt's back." Tears stream down my face.

I'm such a horrible person treating him like he is a speck of dirt while all he did was follow me around like a lost puppy. And now he is gone because of me. Everywhere I turn, someone gets hurt or dies only for breathing the same air. Desperation and self-pity try to sink their clutches on my soul, but I push them away, determined to see this through first. There will be time for despair later.

"Calm down, look." Grunting, Beelzebub jerks his head since his hands are full of still-frozen Eric.

Turning my head, I almost release my hold when I see Colt zooming up with the Trowe in his arms. All the excitement I feel is killed by the sight of the two female demons circling back towards us. They swivel their ugly heads, looking between Beelzebub and Colt. I don't have to wait to see which way they are headed. With both, me and Eric weighing him down, Beelzebub is the easier target because he is moving a lot slower than Colt.

"We have to go down." Beelzebub grunts.

I, on the other hand, am done playing mouse. These abominations are threatening mine and Eric's lives, the life of my sidekick, and these two I reluctantly started to care about. No more hiding and trembling like a frightened little girl. I'm Satan's daughter damn it, and I'm going to show them why Heaven and Hell are after my plump ass. The pep talk worked because I'm not clutching Beelzebub to the point of strangling him.

"Helena, what are you doing?" Alarmed, Beelzebub tries to look at me over his shoulder, unsuccessfully.

"Watch and learn what happens when you push me into a corner." Folding my legs under me, I lift on my knees on top of his back. "Watch and learn."

An awkward chuckle rumbles in his chest, and I feel the vibrations through my knees. The land below us zooms past, blurring into shades of greens and browns. The starless sky sparkles silver from the moon above us, allowing me to see the gruesome faces gunning for us at breakneck speed. Sliding the dagger out and holding it next to my thigh, I push the fingers of my other hand between the soft feathers of Beelzebub's wings. He shivers and gasps, but I ignore him, taking hold of a thicker bone, praying I won't rip the wing off if I get kicked off his back.

"Helena, no!" Colt roars, his face set in firm lines, lips peeled into a snarl as he pushes harder to get to us faster than the two gorgons.

A blind person can see that he won't make it. They don't carry extra weight, slicing through the air like bullets. Their target is me if those creepy glowing eyes are anything to go by. Bracing myself for the impact, my eyes dance in my head, looking for any weakness I might notice to explore.

I see none.

Thick bodies with two sets of breasts, legs like that of the dragon, and two pairs of arms with claw-tipped hands don't give me much hope of surviving this collision. Leaving the doubts to brush off me, I turn my full hunter-honed focus on them. I know I'll be going down, but I'm taking them with me. *At least one,* I amend the closer they get.

Playing along with my insanity, Beelzebub stops flapping his wings, stretching them out and riding the current. That makes me feel more stable, and I lean my upper body forward, waiting unblinking for the gorgons to reach us.

"Playtime," murmuring under my breath, I tighten the grip on the dagger.

They are almost on top of us. The yellowish color of their eyes brightens with hatred and triumph, tightening my gut in knots. I haven't done anything, especially to these two to deserve that. Anger surges through me with so much intensity I'm not sure how I don't erupt like a volcano. I don't have to wonder long because claws reach for me from one blink to the next.

Lashing out with the dagger, I slice through two sets of bellies, my forearm tensing when the blade parts their thick skin. It's almost like punching through water, my shoulder screaming in pain, the action almost ripping my arm out of the socket.

Screeches of pain make my ears ring for long moments when the gorgons teeter in the air, tangling their wings with each other, and go down faster than a rock being dropped. Arms shaking and teeth chattering from the adrenaline cursing through my veins, I watch, fascinated, as they disappear into a barely visible dot.

"I'll be damned." Beelzebub shudders, his head bent down, watching the disappearing gorgons.

"Yeah…" My voice shakes, and I don't dare release my hold on his wing. "You and me both."

Flinching when a gust of wind hits me on the side, Beelzebub growls angrily when I yank on his wing. Colt stops next to us, nostrils flaring and rage twisting his face. Unable to help myself, I grin at him, deepening his scowl.

"You could've died, or been taken." Baring his teeth at me, he looks like a snarling monster.

"Thanks, Mr. Obvious, if you didn't tell me I wouldn't

have noticed." Snapping at him, I pretend like I'm not trying to move my fingers away from Beelzebub's wing.

The picture of the gorgons trying to get me with their claws an inch from my face is burned into my retinas like a permanent feature. Blinking fast only makes me dizzy, not helping at all to clear it. I'm not sure I'll be able to move at all until that happens, so Beelzebub is stuck in this position unless he decides to throw me off his back. Not that I blame him. I can feel a few lose feathers that I've already ripped. If I were in his place, he would've been going down a long time ago.

Colt must've noticed because the scowl is gone. Eyeing me with amusement, he even chuckles, shaking his head. My fingers twitch with the desire to slap him, but I stop when Beelzebub groans again. The big guy sure makes a lot of noises I wasn't aware he was capable of.

Chapter Thirty - One

"He is getting tired." Colt lifts his chin at Beelzebub. "Switch places with the Haltija so we can keep in the air for a little longer. We should be nearing the portal gate soon."

"Unless you are planning on peeling me off him, I'm not sure I can move yet on my own." Deciding that honesty can save me a lot of arguing, I dare him to say something smartass-ish.

His lips lift on one side in a cocky smile, pissing me off before he even opens his mouth. "Not as tough as you…act…"

His words end in a trailed off whisper, his gaze lifting painfully slow over my head. My whole body clenches at the paling of his face when he locks on whatever it is that he is looking at. I really, really don't want to turn around and see what that is. When my skin starts feeling like it'll blister, a groan deflates my chest.

"For fuck's sake. It's that damn dragon, isn't it?" A punch to the head would've been more welcomed.

"Quick, mistress," my sidekick hisses, pushing Colt's arms away like he is not worried that he might be dropped at any second.

"Stop wiggling!" snapping at him, I sneak a fast glance over my shoulder. "Yup, it's that cursed dragon."

"We need to get on the ground, now." I'm proud I managed not to squeak when Beelzebub banks to the side and starts descending.

Colt follows close, I'm sure because he expects me to topple over at any moment. I do my best to ignore his penetrating look while sneaking glances at the shadow of a dragon getting bigger by the second. Even from this far, I can tell it's Leviathan. My mind comes to a screeching halt at that thought.

"It's Leviathan." Waving at Colt with the hand clutching the dagger, excitedly I stab the air with the blade in the direction of the dragon. "Dumbass, it's Leviathan."

Glaring at me, Colt twists his face in anger. "I can see him."

"I know you can see him." Growling through clenched teeth, I glare back. "I mean, it's him. Not a jinn, but the real Leviathan."

"And you know this how? I can't even tell from this far." Beelzebub grunts from underneath me.

"When he attacked Eric, he didn't try to mess with my head." When Colt looks at me like I've lost my mind, I blow breath through pursed lips so I don't stab him for real. "The jinn didn't know that the first time Leviathan saw me, he messed with my head, making me feel like I was burning alive. So, he didn't try mimicking that when he attacked." Colts eyebrows go up at that, making me nod enthusiastically at him. "This one is doing the mind trick again. I think he is making sure we know it's the real him."

"I'm not willing to take that chance she-devil. I'm sorry." Colt doesn't look like he is sorry at all. "We will get on the ground, and we can test the waters from there. Neither, Beelzebub nor I can stand a change in the air at the moment if it comes to a fight. We are both running on fumes."

Begrudgingly, I nod at him. I'm aware I'm acting like a spoiled brat, but after hearing that the portal is near, I can almost smell the smog laden Atlanta air. Being free of this damn place is so close, yet it seems like something will keep happening just to hold me here. I'm determined to not let that happen.

Colt lands first, snatching me around the waist in the air before Beelzebub can fully straighten up. The words I was about to spit at him get stuck in my throat when I see that the golden glow is not around Eric anymore. Slapping Colt's hands away, I rush to my mate.

"He is not awake." Staring at him, I glance quickly at Beelzebub. "Why isn't he awake yet?"

"It'll take him some time to heal from an injury made by a jinn." Colt squeezes my shoulder comfortingly, but I shrug off his touch.

It's not his fault that all this is happening, and I know I'm mostly taking it out on him, but it's not like he was a nice guy and I decided to be a bitch. It'll take a hell of a lot more than running for both our lives for me to remotely trust him.

"How long?" Locking eyes with him, I wait for an exact amount of time because I can feel that I'll freak out. "An hour? Five hours? I need time, Colt. How long?"

"I'm not sure." Something suspiciously like pity passes over his eyes, and I lose my shit.

"You motherfucker!"

Screeching like the gorgons, I jump in his face, poised to stab him with the dagger. Something stops my hand an inch from his chest, right where his heart is. Tense, muscles coiled and ready to snap at a blink of an eye, I can feel myself shaking with rage and fear. Colt doesn't move away or try to block me from invading his personal space. He watches me calmly, unaware I can end his life at whim.

"He is going to wake up." With effort, I push the words through my teeth.

"He will wake up." Calmly, he stays locked with my crazed gaze.

"Because if he doesn't"—Tears prickle my eyes—"I will kill you just so I don't have to be reminded of him every time I look at you."

"I know." His eyes soften at that like a hot poker to my heart. "My brother is a lucky male to have found a female that loves him so fiercely." Guilt crosses his features. "Another thing to envy when it comes to him."

"Speaking of envy," Beelzebub sighs pointing at the sky.

I don't have time to contemplate the words. A shadow blots the silvery glow of the moon, and the next moment, a flash of bright light makes me blink, leaving Leviathan crouched a few feet away from where we are standing.

"Stay where you are." Colt is very much Eric's blood. In his right mind, he pushes me behind his back.

Slamming a hand at the center of his back, I make him stumble a step. "Don't you ever push me behind you, asshole." Swallowing the lump in my throat, I suck air through my nostrils harshly. "Eric does that, not you."

He leaves his mouth open, deciding not to voice whatever he was about to say. I'm grateful for it even when I'll never admit it to him to save my life. Turning to the blond fallen with icy blue eyes, I walk up to where he is standing, watching us like we've all gone nuts.

"Where the hell were you?" He jerks back like I've slapped him, eyes widening at me. "While jinn were impersonating you and we almost died. Where the fuck were you? And more importantly, where is Lucifer?"

After realizing that no enlightenment will come from either Beelzebub or Colt, who are both watching with arms folded over their chests like bodyguards, Leviathan turns the icy gaze back to me. "I was fighting off a horde of gorgons that came out of nowhere." A frown is marring the perfection of his angelic face. "I'm still not certain how they entered the wards, or how I was able to pass them before they almost dropped me on the ground."

"And what? You were there, we just couldn't see you?" Dubiously, I look him up and down.

"As I said" —Narrowing his eyes his nostrils flare— "I chased after them when they tried to flee. When I got back, I found the place empty and no wards to be found. I followed your scents here." Turning to Colt, he bows his head barely. "I don't know where Lucifer is. I thought he was with you even when I didn't catch his scent."

Colt nods back once like that solves all our problems. Men. It'll be a forever mystery how they communicate with each other not using words. My sassy comments die a sudden death when Leviathan continues talking.

"We need to get them through the portal and close the gate. Mammon is coming."

Chapter Thirty-Two

Racing through the dense forest, we stay away from the open paths. I jump over thick gnarled roots and fallen trees, dragging the Trowe along by a tight grip on his hand. The dumb thing will get himself killed if I'm not holding him back. Before we started walking, he kept blabbing about going to meet Mammon on his own to eat his face for hunting his mistress. As endearing as it is that he is so narrow-mindedly protective of me, he started growing on me, and I really don't want him to die.

How things have changed.

I hold Leviathan in my sight since he ended up carrying Eric in a fireman hold regardless of my protests.

According to him, nothing can hurt the Prince of Hell, his words, not mine, while he is in healing sleep. I wanted to stab him in the eye to send him in a healing sleep too and try to see if something can hurt him after that, but Beelzebub stopped me while laughing his ass off. Even Colt released a loud laugh, surprising himself judging by the shocked look on his face.

"We must hurry, mistress," the Trowe hisses, tripping over a root and dangling from my hand, his feet kicking air for a few strides.

"We are moving as fast as we can, Narsi. And watch where you're going. If I trip because of you, I'll kill you myself." Yanking on his arm, I hasten my steps.

"The two of you will tell them where we are if you keep at it," whisper-yelling over his shoulder, Beelzebub is the only one daring to speak to me since he didn't get on my shit list.

He is on it now, and he knows it, too.

We keep at it for what feels like forever, I'm sure it's only been an hour or so in reality. The hairs on the back of my neck stand on end, a sensation of invisible eyes following my every move. This part of Hell has denser woods, the trunks as big as a house making it impossible to see if something is lurking behind them. It might be just paranoia talking, but I get a nudge in my gut that we are missing something.

Beelzebub lifts his hand in the air and we all freeze on the spot. Straining my ears, I try to hear whatever it is that alerted him, but I come up empty. Maybe getting paranoid is not exclusively left to hybrids like myself. The fallen must be susceptible to it, as well.

"Run!"

Even without that word, Leviathan's loud tone would've propelled me forward. The shout tells me it's pointless to be quiet, so I trample everything in my path, cursing loudly at branches that are slapping my arms and face. The rushing sound of my heartbeat is the only thing I can hear as I run as fast as my feet can carry me behind Leviathan. I might be running for my life, but there is no way I'm losing sight of Eric.

Narsi and I are the last to burst out of the thick forest, and I almost bounce off Beelzebub's back. He, Colt, and Leviathan with Eric hanging limply over his shoulders, have stopped a few steps inside the clearing. Peeking around the large guy, I almost run back between the trees.

Mammon is not a fool after all. He set up a trap, waiting for us around the portal consisting of gigantic, furious, horned demons. Fangs dripping saliva gleam in the moonlight on their snarling faces. Muscles bulging, their claws curl and uncurl as if they are already imagining strangling us with bare hands. I jump a foot off the ground when three sets of wings snap open where I'm standing.

Narsi laughs hysterically, gleefully shaking his grinning face at the horde. I must have gone as crazy as he is because a choked laugh comes from me, and all sets off eyes snap in my direction. Even the men that are with me are looking at me strangely.

"We are so screwed," I tell no one in particular.

"You have no idea, my dear." The demons part like the red sea and the one that spoke walks up at the front.

I don't need to be told that this is Mammon. His angelic features, too perfect and symmetrical to be human, would've clued me in enough. But if he is here, then who did Leviathan see coming for us.

"Is it really him?" mumbling under my breath, I nudge Beelzebub.

"I don't have a clue," he murmurs back.

"Hand the girl over, and the three of you may die easy." Mammon flips his long black hair over his broad shoulders like some shampoo commercial. The golden color of his eyes reminds me so much of Raphael's that tears blur my vision. I blink them away.

"If you think I'll just roll over because you said so, you have another thing coming dude." I'm proud that my voice sounds even and steady.

Beelzebub chuckles, shaking his head, and I square my shoulders. Not even the slow grin on Mammon's face can make me balk. I will not show this asshole weakness no matter what. I mean, I'm going to die anyway, which is a reoccurring thought ever since I stepped foot here, so like hell I'm going to let him see that he is getting to me. If I'm not going to make it, it doesn't mean that Eric can't. I have no doubt in my mind that he will avenge my death and find a way to kill this jerk.

"No matter what, get Eric through that portal." My words are barely above a whisper, and I'm praying that Beelzebub heard me. The way his body stills, I'm pretty sure he did.

"Get the girl through the portal at all costs." Leviathan, the killjoy that he is, destroys my plans of glorious death when he opens his mouth.

Everyone moves at the same time, not giving me time to light a fire under his ass for speaking on my behalf like I'm a child. Roars are deafening when the horde descends on us from all sides. We were surrounded while standing clueless, chatting with Mammon.

Turning back to back we face them. In their haste to get to me, they mindlessly push each other out of the way, helping us slightly with it. Falling into the routine of a fight, I join in, punching, kicking, and stabbing anything that doesn't belong to the three men and sidekick fighting by my side. Screams replace the furious roars as one by one the almost feral demons drop on the ground in the puddles of their own blood.

I grind my teeth, not daring to utter a sound when my skin gets shredded by claws and horns. Angry grunts and growls tell me my companions are not faring better either. I watch in disbelief when my sidekick turns into a killing machine, his mouth full of sharp teeth opening impossibly wide and biting off limbs every chance he gets.

The distraction costs me dearly when a horn as thick as my shin nails me in the thigh. Slicing my hand down, the blade glides through the demon's neck like a knife through butter, spraying me with the hot gushing of blood. Swaying slightly on my feet, I almost faceplant on the ground, but a large hand wraps around my arm, stopping me.

"We must push through. She won't last much longer." I think it's Colt that speaks but my ears are full with the sound of a freight train coming at me at full speed.

"I can fight." Slurring my words with a tongue too thick for my mouth, I push the hand away. I try to anyway.

"I know you can, she-devil, but I wouldn't dare face my brother if anything happens to you." The nickname confirms that it's Colt holding me standing.

I feel his body jerk before I hear the pained grunt that he tries to hide. He keeps moving, Beelzebub and Leviathan guarding our backs and my sidekick clearing a path towards the sparkling gate ahead. It's so close I can almost reach out and touch it. To my horror, I see Leviathan using Eric's body like a weapon, swinging around and knocking demons away from us. Blood is dripping from Eric's arms and legs, proving the dragon asshole lied about not getting hurt while in healing sleep. When a giant demon resembling a bull charges Leviathan with his crazed eyes locked on my mate, my scream makes everyone around me drop on their knees, covering their ears.

Colt pushes off the ground first, snatching me again and bolting for the portal. Digging my heels in, I fight his pull, not daring to leave Eric behind no matter what.

"I will send him after you, I swear it on my life." He puts his body weight into it, almost picking me off the ground. Looking around us, dread settles in my stomach like lead.

"What about the four of you?" My question stops Colt unlike anything else would've. "They will kill you if I'm not here. At the moment, they're only trying to get to me."

Clenching his jaw, he recovers from the shock fast. "We'll be fine, we can fly."

I would've believed him if I didn't see their bloodied wings, the tips dragging behind them on the blood-soaked dirt. Nodding jerkily, I allow him to pull me closer to the portal, hanging back just enough for Beelzebub and Leviathan to be near. Convinced that I believe him, Colt reaches the Trowe at the portal. Beelzebub and Leviathan form a living wall between me and the still charging demons.

"Grab Eric, and I'll go first." Limply, I push on Colt's arm, showing him I barely have any strength to stay standing.

With one last look to make sure I stay put, he takes the few steps to the other fallen, reaching for his brother. Knowing I only have a few precious seconds of time to execute my plan, I rub my hands over my bleeding wounds. My sidekick watches me with his mouth open, I don't doubt aware of what I'm planning to do.

"Don't you dare judge me." Snapping at him makes the three men turn around to look at me.

Darting at them, smudging my blood anywhere I can reach, praying that I'm not making the biggest mistake in the history of humankind, I face them all.

"If you don't walk through that portal this second, I'm letting Mammon take me wherever he wants." Dancing away from Colt when he tries to snatch me, I inch away from the portal. "Enough people have died on my behalf. You either go through the portal or get the hell out of my face." Narsi throws himself around my leg, rubbing my blood on his face and bolts through the portal like an arrow.

"Fucking Heltija," Colt snarls, but I can see the decision made on his face.

All three of them close rank around me, and I grab hold of one wing from each in one hand, and Eric's dangling hand in the other. With one last look at the terrifying sight around us, we jump through the portal together. When the feeling of my body being sucked in through a thin straw overtakes my mind, I dare dream that we find a better situation when we pop out in Atlanta.

A girl can only hope.

To be continued

FROM THE AUTHOR

Dear reader,

We went through another chapter of Helena and Eric's story. Few questions were not answered, but I promise it's all going to come together at the end. The Devil in Disguise is almost ready and you'll be able to continue the adventure with our sassy girl. She came a long way but there is so much more in store for her. I hope you enjoyed reading it as much as I'm having a blast while writing the story.

If you haven't joined the newsletter, follow the link. I've been working on an exclusive story as a prologue for my new trilogy, the novella will be available only to my subscribers. You don't want to miss it, I'm totally in love with it!

Please consider leaving a review, they are like hugs to us authors and we appreciate each and every single one. Even if there was something you didn't like in the book. And, come chat with me in my readers group on Facebook. We are very much alike, you and I. I'm a reader as well, so we can swap stories. Or, just talk about what else you would love to see in any of the series already out on Amazon. :)

Newsletter sign up

Reader’s group join here

May the odds be always in your favor!

Maya xxx

ALSO BY MAYA DANIELS

Semiramis series-Urban Fantasy/PNR:

Who am I - Prequel to the Semiramis series

Semiramis Awakened Book 1

Semiramis Reborn Book 2

Semiramis The Vessel Book 3

Stand alone-Dark Fantasy romance/ Mythology:

The Cursed Kingdom

Hidden Portals trilogy- PNR:

Venus Trap Book 1

The First Secret Book 2

The Obsidian Throne- coming soon

The Broken Halos series- PNR/Urban Fantasy:

The Devil is in the Details Book 1

Speak of the Devil Book 2

Encounter with the Devil Book 3

The Devil in Disguise Book 4

To look the Devil in the eye Book 5 - coming soon

New Blood Rising series- Dark PNR

Risorgimento-Rebirth Book 1

Rovesciamento-Overthrown Book 2

Riconoscimento-Recognition Book 3 - coming soon

Printed in Great Britain
by Amazon